Lucas Lightfoot and the FIRE CRYSTAL

Readers love

Lucas Lightfoot and the Fire Crystal

"*Lucas Lightfoot and the Fire Crystal* is a lovely tale about the adventures of Lucas and his chameleon. As a teacher, I have enjoyed this story immensely because it has a positive message and is relatable to my students. Sharing it with my students has opened the door for interesting, deep conversations. My students find the story amazing and fun!"

Crystal Romans
5th Grade Teacher, Herriman, UT

"I was hooked from the start with the vivid descriptions and the intrigue of a talking chameleon guiding the young hero. As a parent and teacher, I was captured by the action and integrity. The book speaks to children. It is relatable. Kids love powers and super heroes. Better yet, parents and teachers are attracted to this young book hero who has powers that are activated and strengthened by virtues. The author has a knack for kid connection. This book is an adventurous treat for children and adults alike. Find a young friend and read it together."

Sandi Moore
3rd Grade Teacher, Templeton, CA

"My students used adjectives like "hypnotizing, mysterious, and superb" to describe the story. Young readers will be captivated by the plot of the story, but they won't fail to recognize that the goodness in Lucas's heart is the true source of his power. This book is perfectly suited for the minds and hearts of children."

Cindy Miller
3rd Grade Teacher, Templeton, CA

"I love the positive messages about virtue, attitude and choices. It's perfect and my kids love it. In fact, I love when I hear them talk about why it's good to be good in the way we just read."

Darren E., Santa Monica, CA

"The book is very exciting with good characters and an intriguing plot. Even if there wasn't a deeper meaning to everything, it would still stand on its own. Important skills and character traits are taught through the experiences of the main character. It is magical."

Tim M.,Templeton, CA

"This is a very delightful and amazing book. The story line is captivating and very original. Our 8-year-old son has reread the book five times and I overheard him say that he and friends at school are playing Lucas Lightfoot on the play ground and using "their power" for good."

Lenny Z., Paso Robles, CA

Lucas Lightfoot

Lightfoot

AND THE

Fire Crystal

HUGO HASELHUHN
LUKE COWDELL

New York

Lucas Lightfoot and the FIRE CRYSTAL

Published in New York, New York, by Morgan James Publishing. Morgan James and The Entrepreneurial Publisher are trademarks of Morgan James, LLC. www.MorganJamesPublishing.com

The Morgan James Speakers Group can bring authors to your live event. For more information or to book an event visit The Morgan James Speakers Group at www.TheMorganJamesSpeakersGroup.com.

Shelfie

A **free** eBook edition is available
with the purchase of this print book.

CLEARLY PRINT YOUR NAME ABOVE IN UPPER CASE

Instructions to claim your free eBook edition:
1. Download the Shelfie app for Android or iOS
2. Write your name in **UPPER CASE** above
3. Use the Shelfie app to submit a photo
4. Download your eBook to any device

ISBN 978-1-63047-783-7 paperback
ISBN 978-1-63047-784-4 eBook

Title Font: Romance Fatal Serif
© Juan Casco, Used with permission

Cover illustration by:
Emily Tjomsland

Cover Design by:
Rachel Lopez
www.r2cdesign.com

In an effort to support local communities and raise awareness and funds, Morgan James Publishing donates a percentage of all book sales for the life of each book to Habitat for Humanity Peninsula and Greater Williamsburg

Get involved today, visit
www.MorganJamesBuilds.com

Habitat for Humanity®
Peninsula and
Greater Williamsburg
Building Partner

To all of the children who find it easy to imagine themselves in the magical world of adventure with Lucas and Hailey.

To all of the adults who read with their children, so they can relive their childhood fantasies through these adventures.

To all young readers and those who are young at heart who believe they can make a difference in the lives of children.

Contents

Preface

Why do I write? It began as a way to help a grandson achieve a dream. As I continue to write, it is because I want to improve the lives of children. Throughout the story, my goal is to teach the importance of choice and accountability, the value of learning and improving the mind, importance of attitude and belief in one's ability to help others. Integrity and honesty are still valuable traits to develop and hold dear. There is value in love, understanding and gratitude in our lives. These values are critical for a rising generation that is bombarded with anti-heroes that exemplify the opposite traits of selfishness, falsehoods, power-seeking and bullying. The lessons are communicated within the conversations and actions of the characters while the reader is drawn into the excitement that comes with the challenges and adventures in the story. I marvel as I watch children read the story and get excited as they are caught up in the adventure and excitement. One of the greatest compliments I have yet heard about the book: The children are "playing Lucas Lightfoot" on the playground. If I can enlighten a child and take them on an adventure they enjoy again and again, I feel successful in my writing. Why do I write? I write to change the world, one child at a time.

Acknowledgements

First and foremost, I want to thank my grandson, Luke Cowdell, who, at the age of seven, had a desire to write a "chapter book" and secondly, my daughter, Heather Cowdell, for having the audacity to encourage her son to accomplish his dreams. Because of Luke, I have been able to check off another item on my bucket list. When Luke told his mother of his desire, she assured him that "Grandpa Hugo" could help him. How could I say no to my grandson? Many of the ideas and accomplishments of the hero in our story are from the mind of Luke. He told me about the hero and I provided the road, created the travelers and painted the scenery along the road they traveled.

I am thankful to my daughter Heather, who is the artistic talent behind the illustrations that help bring the story to life through pictures. I am grateful to Emily Tjomsland who captured the essence of the story in the beautiful digital painting for the cover art.

I appreciate the input from two special school teachers, Nicole Delbar, who provided insight early in the writing, and Janice Paxman, who ensured I followed correct formatting and punctuation. I am especially thankful to Patricia Alexander for her careful editing to create a polished manuscript. Patricia has been a tremendous help in bringing clarity and honesty to my writing and to my characters. She has a keen ear and listens carefully for the emotions, sentence structure and the appropriate language for the intended reader. Working with Patricia has helped me take a good story and make it great.

I am grateful to Mary, Ethan, Mason, Chase, Kyle, Lucas and Audrey. They are my young readers who read to me, chapter by chapter, to ensure the story matched their reading level and provided generous feedback.

I am thankful to Scott Frishman who took a chance on me and recommended this book to Morgan James Publishing.

I am grateful to the third grade teachers, Ms. Miller and Mrs. Moore, who were cheerleaders for Lucas Lightfoot and believed in the value of reading his adventures to their students. These two teachers are so inspiring, they have found their way into characters in *Lucas Lightfoot and the Sun Stone.*

And finally, I am so grateful to the love of my life, Lydia, my wife and eternal companion. She encouraged me throughout the writing and reminded me that the readers will be children, and to write for them. I trusted her with a red pen in her hand and she proved invaluable in editing the story.

Although some of the elements in this story may appear to be biographical with a tiny thread of truth woven into the story, it is a work of fiction, and all characters described are fictitious. Any resemblance to real persons, living, dead or anywhere in between is purely coincidental.

ONE

Lucas Meets Prescott

We might meet by chance,
but we are friends by choice.

Lucas slammed on his brakes and skidded to a stop as he swerved his bike off the sidewalk and onto the grass. "What was that?" he asked his dad. "It moved!"

Lucas pointed to what he thought was a green stick just inches away from the black skid mark. Whatever it was, it turned its head and looked right at Lucas. Lucas had narrowly missed running over a small lizard whose tiny scales reflected in the sunlight like emerald crystals with ruby tattoos. It was definitely the strangest creature he had ever seen.

Lucas's dad carefully picked up the reptile. "It looks like a lizard," he said. "In fact, it's a chameleon. Although, this is strange, I have never seen a chameleon wearing a collar. It must belong to someone, but the collar doesn't show a name, just these strange symbols."

"Can we keep it, Dad?" asked Lucas.

"Let's take it into the house and keep it safe first. Before we decide whether or not to keep it, we need to see if it belongs to one of the neighbors."

Lucas knew they should check with the neighbors, but he hoped that they would not find the owner. After all, who would let such a beautiful creature escape?

Lucas lived on a quiet street in Tustin, California, about ten miles south of Disneyland. His was a dead end street, so most of the cars driving by belonged to the local residents. Lucas recognized most of the people in the neighborhood and his parents waved to almost everybody. There was a creek that ran behind Lucas's house, which usually had enough water to make it difficult to cross on foot and stay dry. In the winter, during the heavy rains, the water flowed dangerously fast, so his mom did not allow Lucas to play in the creek.

Once the chameleon was settled in a cardboard box in Lucas's room, Lucas and his dad walked to the neighboring houses and showed a picture of the chameleon to everyone who was at home. After they got to the end of the block, they decided that the lizard had probably not gone that far so they crossed the street and walked on the other side.

With still no success, they crossed back to their side of the street. After a few houses, Lucas walked up to a house with a rocking horse on the porch and rang the doorbell—and prayed that no one was home!

A tall woman answered the door. She had silver hair, deep green eyes, and a very kind face. Lucas thought he saw a hint of recognition in her face and wondered if he had seen her somewhere before. Her face actually seemed to glow when she smiled and asked, "Can I help you?"

"Did you lose a chameleon?" Lucas asked, holding up a photograph of the green and red creature.

The woman's eyes lit up. "Where did you find him?" she asked.

Lucas told her about the near miss on the sidewalk in front of his house and explained that the chameleon was at their home.

"My name is Katrina," said the woman, "and that chameleon belonged to my son, but it escaped from its cage over a year ago. I'm very surprised that it's still alive! About two years ago, my son was given the chameleon by a friend who owed him money. Supposedly, it was a "magical" lizard and worth much more than the five-hundred dollars he was owed. My son did not expect to get his money, so he took the chameleon, never once believing it was magical."

"Is it really a magical chameleon?" asked Lucas with excitement.

"My son didn't believe that there was any magic in that chameleon, but now I'm not so sure." And then with a smile, she said, "How could he live on his own for so long if he didn't have a little magic in him?"

"I'm glad we found you," said Lucas's father. "We'll go get the chameleon and bring him back to you."

Lucas's shoulders drooped as he looked at the ground. He had hoped to keep the chameleon, but now he would have to give it back.

"Oh no! My son has moved to the east coast, and I no longer have the cage."

Then, looking at Lucas, Katrina asked, "Would you be willing to give the chameleon a good home and take really good care of him?"

Lucas's face split into a big grin. "Oh, you bet! Please! Please, Dad! Can I keep him?"

"We'll have to get your mother to agree, but leave that to me, I think I can work a little magic of my own," said Lucas's dad.

"It would make me very happy if you could give the chameleon a good home," added Katrina. "Before you go, I think I still have a few books on caring for chameleons. Would you like them?"

"Sure!" said Lucas and his dad at the same time.

While she was gone, Lucas said, "We should give the chameleon a name."

"I agree. Since you found him, you should choose the name. Do you have any ideas?"

Lucas thought for a while. "It needs to be a good name, because this is a very special chameleon, maybe even magical. Lizards like to warm themselves in the sun. I was doing some homework this week and learned about a place in Arizona called Prescott. Since Prescott is a warm town, I think we should name him Prescott."

"That sounds like a great name for a special chameleon," said his dad.

The woman returned and handed two books to Lucas. "Be sure to read about how to care for and feed him because chameleons are not native to North America," she said. "Most chameleons come from Africa or Madagascar, and this particular breed lives in the forest, so he likes trees, leaves, and branches."

They thanked Katrina again, and as they turned to go, she said, "I wish you luck understanding the symbols on his collar. Maybe that's where magic is. Oh, and I forgot to tell you, Lucas, the chameleon's name is Prescott. But since he's yours now, you can name him anything you like."

Lucas and his dad looked at each other with wide-eyed amazement, and then back at the woman, who just smiled, waved and closed the door.

"Wow! Did you hear that?" said Lucas. "It's like I read her mind."

Lucas and his dad hurried home to share the news. And silently, Lucas determined that he was going to find the magic in Prescott.

That afternoon, after reading some of the basics about caring for a chameleon, Lucas and his family went to the local pet store. Lucas read that chameleons love to eat crickets. When a chameleon is on the hunt for food, it may sit quietly and wait for its prey to come near, or it may move slowly and quietly along a branch or the ground. It has funny mitten-like feet to give it a firm grip on a branch, and its two eyes turn in different directions at once, looking for the slightest movement for food. No other animal on earth has eyes and feet like a chameleon.

They bought a cage with a lamp and some crickets for Prescott. Since lizards are cold-blooded, they need heat from the sun or from a light to keep them warm. They decorated Prescott's new home with some branches and leaves from a tree in their yard and a flat bowl for water. They released five crickets into the cage and watched Prescott to see what he would do.

Lucas had read that when a chameleon spots an insect or other prey, its eyes lock in on the target. After taking careful aim, the chameleon shoots out its super-long tongue, which is usually longer than its body. The tip of the tongue is wet and shaped like a suction cup. When the tongue smacks against the prey, the prey sticks to it and the tongue snaps back into the chameleon's open mouth.

Everyone was watching closely to see if Prescott was hungry. They didn't have to wait very long. Prescott stood very still until a cricket came close to him. His tongue shot out of his mouth and the cricket became dinner in less than a second! Lucas's little sister, Madison, squealed with delight and clapped her hands when she saw the long tongue shoot out and the cricket disappear into Prescott's mouth. Within a short time, all of the crickets were gone and Prescott looked directly at Lucas as if to say,

"Thank you. I was very hungry."

Lucas's little brother, Gavin, wanted to take Prescott out of his cage and play with him, but their dad had to remind all of the kids that a chameleon was not like a dog or cat. They should not expect to play fetch with it like a dog with a ball or pet it like a cat. Although direct contact with Prescott needed

to be limited, they could let Prescott out on warm days and watch him explore in the grass.

That night, the cage for Prescott was set up in Lucas's room near his bed. He had had a very exciting day. He almost ran over a chameleon, and now the chameleon was his pet, a gift from Katrina. As he thought about the woman that gave him Prescott, Lucas remembered where he had seen her. Oddly, she was in a dream he had had several nights ago. He didn't remember much about the dream except for her kind face, soft voice and her beautiful green eyes. He did remember that she said, "We have been waiting for you Lucas."

Suddenly, it occurred to him, that as he and his dad were leaving her house, she called him Lucas. He had not told her his name! Just thinking about that gave him goose bumps and he pulled the covers up to his neck. Lucas drifted off to sleep thinking about Prescott.

Little did he know that finding Prescott would change his life in ways he could never imagine. To those who knew Lucas Lightfoot, he appeared to be an average boy from an average family living in Southern California. But that had all changed today. To the Lightfoot family, it would be a day long remembered as the day Lucas met Prescott... and the beginning of a new life for Lucas.

TWO

Surprise Awakening

---

*Allow yourself a few surprises everyday
and enjoy the wonders around you.*

The first thing Lucas did when he woke up the next morning was to rush over to Prescott's cage and say, "Good morning!"

Prescott turned both eyes toward Lucas, winked one eye and stuck out his tongue, wiggling it slightly. Lucas thought that was really weird, as if Prescott was saying good morning to him. At that moment, Lucas remembered the strange dream he had and he went into his parents' room.

"I had a really strange dream last night," said Lucas. "I dreamed that Prescott called me by my name, and thanked me for saving his life, giving him a nice warm home, and giving him delicious crickets to eat. Isn't that a weird dream?"

"Oh, not that weird," said his mother. "Yesterday was definitely exciting enough to have caused you to dream about Prescott."

Lucas agreed and went back to his room and pulled out the books he had gotten from Katrina. As he looked through them, he saw that there were a lot more varieties of chameleons than he had thought. He decided that Prescott was the most beautiful type. He figured out from the pictures that Prescott was a *veiled chameleon* from the rain forest in Madagascar. His green and red coloring was perfect for living in the forest.

Lucas knew that chameleons changed colors to match their surroundings. In his reading though, he found out that chameleons choose to hang out where their normal, "everyday" colors match their environment. So green chameleons usually live among green leaves, and brown ones may live on the ground. This helps hide them from predators as well as making it easier for them to surprise their prey.

Chameleons may turn a lighter color to cool down or darker to warm up because dark colors take in more heat from the sun. Chameleons may also change color when they become frightened, angry, or feel stressed. Lucas smiled when remembering that his Grandpa Jack sometimes turned red in the face when he got stressed.

As Lucas read more, he learned that chameleons also use their colors to communicate with one another. One color may mean, "Stay away from me!" A different color may mean, "Do you want to be my friend?"

When he got to the end of the book, he was surprised to find a small envelope taped to the inside back cover. He opened it and found a curious-looking thin disk inside. The disk was about two and half inches in diameter and about the thickness of the old silver dollar his Grandpa Jack had given him. It was cool to the touch like some kind of metal. It appeared to be two pieces. There was an inner flat disk and an outer ring that was raised slightly. The inner disk was red with a hole in the middle and it had a small triangle-like pointer. The outer ring was green and was able to spin around the inner disk since both pieces were locked together. The outer ring was divided into eight sections with a line dividing them. Each section had a strange symbol that Lucas thought he had seen before, but where? Then he remembered: They were the same symbols that were on Prescott's collar!

He turned the disk over to look at the backside and saw the following words engraved in a circular shape on the outer ring: "VIRTUE UNLOCKS POWER"

Lucas was not certain about the meaning of VIRTUE, so he decided to look it up. He found three definitions:

1. *Conformity to a standard of right or particular moral excellence*
2. *Quality or power of a thing*
3. *Manly strength or courage*

Which definition was right for the ring? There was clearly only one thing to do: Lucas went to ask his mother, who was in the kitchen.

"Mom, I have a question. What does "virtue" mean?"

"Well, it means to have high morals or honorable standards. Do you remember how we've talked about making good decisions and choosing between right and wrong? If you make the right choice, then you feel good about it and you feel good about yourself. You also show others you have high standards and can be trusted," replied his mother.

Lucas thought about that for a little bit and then asked,

"How does virtue unlock power?"

His mother was a little surprised that her ten-year-old son was asking such grown-up questions.

"What exactly do you mean? Where are you getting these questions?"

Lucas was concerned that the disk he found in the back of the book might be valuable, and he might have to return it to Katrina. However, she was insistent that Lucas take Prescott, and she DID give him the book. He decided to let his mom in on his discovery.

Lucas said, "Look at this Mom."

He reached into his pocket and pulled out the red and green disk and handed it to his mother.

"I found this in the back of one of the books that lady gave me. It looks like it may be valuable. The markings on the front are the same as on Prescott's collar, and the outer ring spins around the inside. But what's really strange is the writing on the back."

Lucas's mother turned over the disk and read the words, slowly turning the disk as she read: "VIRTUE UNLOCKS POWER."

"You're right," said his mother. "It is very strange. I wonder if the woman who gave you Prescott knew about this disk. You and your dad should probably go ask her about it and see if she can tell you what it is and if she wants it back."

Lucas hoped that Katrina didn't want it back. Maybe she could tell him if the magic was in the ring. When his dad came home, Lucas showed him the disk and his dad agreed that they should talk with the woman again. Lucas and his father walked up to the house with the rocking horse on the porch. They knocked and heard the sound of little feet running toward the door. A young woman opened the door and there were two little girls standing beside her.

"Yes, can I help you?" asked the woman.

Lucas's father asked, "Is Katrina here?"

"I'm sorry. There is no Katrina who lives here," said the young mother.

Lucas and his father looked at each other, very confused.

"We were here last Saturday afternoon and spoke with a woman named Katrina who had lost a chameleon that my son found. She had silver hair and green eyes," explained Lucas's father.

"Oh, the person you are describing sounds like Katherine. She sold us this home about a year ago. We were gone all this weekend, so she couldn't have talked with you," explained the young mother.

"Do you know where she is living or how we can contact her?" asked Lucas's dad.

"I'm sorry. I don't know where she is living now," replied the young mother with a puzzled smile.

Not knowing how to explain how they met Katrina as she stood in this house while the owners were gone, Lucas's father said,

"I guess—I guess we made a mistake. Thanks for the information. By the way, my name is Andrew and this is my son Lucas and we live five houses up the street."

"Oh, it's nice to meet you. And I'm sorry I couldn't be of more help," said the woman.

Lucas and his father had a lot more questions than answers as they walked home.

"I guess that means I can keep the Power Ring since there is no one to return it to," said Lucas.

His father agreed and said, "With Katrina gone, I guess we'll never know what the symbols on the ring mean. By the way, why did you call it a Power Ring?"

"I don't know," replied Lucas. "I guess because it has the word "Power" on it."

For the next few nights Lucas dreamed that Prescott was talking to him. He dreamed that Prescott was telling him about the symbols on the Power Ring.

"One symbol represents the power to stop time; another, the power to be invisible; and another, the power to move things with your mind."

In his dream, Lucas had the thought, *"but what about the purpose of the other symbols?"*

Prescott answered, *"The purpose of the other symbols will be revealed if you meet the challenges ahead."*

Still dreaming, Lucas heard Prescott say, *"Do you think that finding me on the sidewalk was by chance? Do you think that speaking with Katrina was also by some accident? No, Lucas. I chose you because you are special. I want to teach you about the power of the ring because you have a good heart. But remember, Lucas, this power can only be used for good and unselfish reasons. If you try to use this power to control others or for selfish desires, it simply will not work! Or it may work in unexpected ways, so be careful. Remember, you must serve others. With this power comes the responsibility to use it wisely and it can only be used with virtue."*

Lucas bolted awake and jumped out of bed. It was still dark outside and the red numbers on the clock showed that it was 3:45 in the morning. Lucas turned on the small desk lamp, lifted the cover on the cage, and looked at Prescott. Prescott was looking directly at Lucas.

Lucas quietly said, "I was having a dream that you were talking to me." No sooner were the words out of his mouth, than Lucas heard a voice in his head.

"I was talking with you! I was telling you about the Power Ring and some of the symbols."

Lucas fell back on the bed, rubbed his eyes, and then pinched himself to make sure he was not dreaming. In his mind he heard Prescott's voice again.

"Lucas, I am a chameleon and yes, my name is Prescott. You can pinch yourself all you want, but you are most definitely awake and we have a lot to talk about."

THREE

The Power Ring

Give someone adversity to test his strength.
Give him power to test his character.

For the rest of the night, Prescott told Lucas the history behind the Power Ring and how Prescott became the guardian. Lucas listened to Prescott's voice inside his head. He was speaking as if they were his own thoughts. And when Lucas had a question, all he had to do was think about it.

Prescott began, *"I am sure you would like to know how a talking chameleon came into your life. Lucas, I have been watching you for some time. I knew that my last caretaker did not deserve the ring and began looking for someone who would value this gift and be worthy of its power. I have seen how you treat your family and friends and even those who are unkind to you. When I crawled onto the sidewalk in front of your bicycle, I knew you would stop.*

"Let me tell you a little about my self. You might be surprised to know that I am almost one hundred years old. My original home was in the rain forest in Madagascar and my keeper was a shaman."

Lucas interrupted, "What is a shaman?"

"A shaman is a very wise man. He taught me and many others the skills I will now teach you."

"Wait a minute," said Lucas. "Do you mean there are a lot of chameleons in the world with this power?"

"Actually, there is only one other chameleon. There are other animals and birds that have been trained, but most who have received this power are humans."

"How many people have you taught?" asked Lucas.

"It has been many years since I was trained by the shaman. You will be number seventy-two, but it is becoming difficult to find those with a heart like yours Lucas. Some I have trained are now training others. Unfortunately, there are others I trained who have lost their power because their hearts turned dark and hard."

"Do I know any of these people who have a Power Ring?" asked Lucas.

"If there are others with this power, it is up to them to tell you and not me. Now, what was I saying?"

"You were telling me about the shaman," replied Lucas.

"Right. Many years ago the shaman created the Power Ring from some very rare metals that have unique properties. You could think of the metals in the ring like a magnet that pulls energy toward it. Once the shaman had completed the rings so they turned freely within one another, he gave it power from the crystal in the center."

Lucas interrupted, "But there is no crystal in the inner disk."

Prescott replied, *"Very clever. You did notice that the crystal is indeed missing, and I will need your help to replace it.*

"The Power Ring operates by the power of your virtue or goodness, and by the power within the crystal. You turn the pointer on the center disk toward the desired power and squeeze the crystal. The crystal that fits into the center ring is a Fire Crystal and looks like a ruby. It was found near my home in Madagascar and cut by the shaman. The shape, the cuts and even the polished surfaces on the Fire Crystal are important. There is a natural frequency within the structure of the crystal that makes it vibrate. When the vibration of the crystal is combined with the rare metals of the ring, it becomes a source of power.

When virtue and positive thoughts are added to the Power Ring, a greater power is generated that you can control and direct. The energy from the crystal will increase your will power, courage and inner strength. It has a powerful positive quality and will actually magnify your positive thoughts. The power however is cancelled by negative thoughts."

Prescott could see that Lucas was trying to understand everything he was explaining and paused so Lucas could consider the connection between the Power Ring and one's thoughts. Prescott continued speaking in Lucas's mind.

"As you use the Power Ring and develop a connection to it, you will find that you no longer need to turn the pointer or squeeze the crystal. You will develop the power of telekinesis to turn the pointer and squeeze the crystal with your mind."

Lucas interrupted again and asked, "What is te-le-ki-ne-sis?"

"Telekinesis is the power to move objects with just the power of your thought and is just one of the powers I will teach you."

"Does each symbol represent some power?" asked Lucas.

"Yes," replied Prescott. *"To start your training, I will tell you about three of the symbols and the power linked to each. The first power you may use is telekinesis. At first you will be able to move small items like pencils or toys. The symbol is the*

Three Arrows pointing right to remind you to do what's right."

Prescott continued, *"The second power will be the ability to stop time. That power is represented by the Double-T with the circle above it. You may use this to protect someone from injury or to give you more time to accomplish something.*

"With the third power, you will be able to become invisible. That is the symbol that looks like a Double-S."

"Cool," thought Lucas, *"I will be able to hide from Mom and Dad and play tricks on my little brother and sister."*

Lucas heard Prescott in his mind. *"These powers are not to be used foolishly."*

Lucas replied in a whisper, "Oops! I forgot you can hear my thoughts."

Lucas didn't know when he went back to sleep but he jumped out of bed when the alarm went off.

He looked over at Prescott and thought, *"Was I dreaming?"*

Immediately he heard Prescott's voice in his head, *"You were not dreaming, and you need to keep our secret to yourself until the time is right to tell others."*

Lucas agreed and excitedly went off to get ready for school. Later that morning, Lucas was sitting at his desk in class, deep in thought about the conversations with Prescott and about the Power Ring.

"Lucas. Lucas!"

He snapped out of his daydreaming and answered without thinking, "Yes, Prescott!"

His teacher said, "That's a good guess, but the capital of Arizona is Phoenix."

Some of the other children were giggling, but Kevin, the class bully, was laughing the hardest. This really bothered Lucas, and he wished he could use some of the powers to teach Kevin a lesson. Then he remembered that the Power Ring could only be used for good so he let go of his anger. Lucas did not like Kevin and tried to stay out of his way. Kevin was bigger than all of the other kids and he used that to his advantage.

Lauren Harrison, Lucas's teacher, loved teaching and the opportunity it gave her to nourish and inspire her students. Miss Harrison looked much younger than she really was. The bounce in her step and the enthusiasm in her voice were more often seen in women much younger. She had brown hair that curled inward on her shoulders, sparkling white teeth and a big welcoming smile. Her soft hazel eyes invited trust and showed a loving concern. She was not like any other teacher and Lucas liked being in her class. She made school fun, but even better was sitting next to his friend Hailey. She was pretty with her blond hair and blue eyes, but she was really smart too. Lucas found it easy to talk with her and thought there was something special about her.

There was a light in her eyes that made her stand out from others. She was very curious and asked many questions until she found the answer. She had the ability to see things going on around her and understand how to solve problems. Lucas wanted to share his secret with her, but he knew he needed to do as Prescott instructed. Besides, she might think he was weird telling her about a magical talking chameleon. Yet, Lucas had a feeling that someday he *would* be able to share his secret with Hailey.

FOUR

The Fire Crystal

The road ahead is best traveled
when our companion is one we trust.

When Lucas got home from school, he went to his room to check on Prescott. Prescott was sitting very still on a branch with his back to Lucas. Without turning his head, Prescott opened his eyes and rotated them backward to look at Lucas and said,

"So you think I have funny eyes."

"Oops," said Lucas, "I keep forgetting you can hear my thoughts."

"That is okay," said Prescott, *"Because I am different, that makes me special and unique."*

Lucas's mother called from the hall. "Lucas, who are you talking to?"

Lucas replied, "I'm just talking to Prescott."

"Okay. Let me know when he starts talking back to you," said his mother with a smile. "That would really make him a special chameleon!"

"Really, Mom?" said Lucas, "A talking chameleon?"

His mom asked, "When you said, 'I keep forgetting you can hear my thoughts,' what did you mean?"

Lucas heard Prescott in his head, *"Just tell your mother that you are playing an imaginary game with me, and then ask your mother if she can make a special shoulder pack so you can carry me. I have a special task for you and I need you to take me somewhere."*

"Oh, you heard that?" said Lucas to his mom. "I was just playing an imaginary game with Prescott. Hey Mom, can you make a shoulder pack so I can carry Prescott with me? He wants me—I mean, um, I want to take him with me sometimes when I go out," said Lucas.

Lucas's mother thought this behavior was a little strange, but decided to play along and asked, "What kind of pack do you want?"

Lucas could hear Prescott say, *"Like Uncle Brett's."*

"Well, maybe you could make it something like the one-shoulder pack that Uncle Brett has," answered Lucas.

"Make the outer covering with mesh so I can breathe."

"And Mom, can you make the outer covering with mesh so I can—I mean, so Prescott can breathe," said Lucas in response to his prompting.

"And please make it green so I cannot be easily seen."

"And can you make it green like Prescott? That way people won't know that I have him."

That night Lucas asked if he could go to bed early. He didn't tell his mother that he was up half the night listening to a chameleon because she might think that he was taking this imaginary game too far.

Again in the middle of the night, Lucas heard Prescott invading his sleep.

"Lucas. Lucas, wake up! I need you to hear what I have to say. I heard your thoughts at dinner when your mother asked about your day. I know you wanted to tell her what you would like to do to Kevin, but the power can only be used for good."

"Yes, I know," said Lucas sleepily, "Did you wake me up to tell me that?"

"Yes, because it is important. Also, I need you to take me to where I have hidden the Fire Crystal. We can go after school to get it," said Prescott.

"But you said it was in the creek," said Lucas, "and my mom doesn't want me to go to the creek."

"*Leave your mom to me,*" said Prescott. "*Just come home right after school. Now go back to sleep.*"

☼ ☼ ☼

The next day Lucas came home right after school and was just getting ready to ask his mom if he could take Prescott to the creek when she asked him a question.

"Lucas, can you do me a favor? Gavin kicked his ball over the fence and into the creek behind the house. Can you go up the street to the footpath bridge and go down into the creek and get the ball?"

It hadn't rained for awhile, so she knew the water in the creek wasn't too deep. Lucas was surprised that his mom would ask him to go to the creek and then he remembered that Prescott said, "*Leave your mom to me.*"

Lucas asked, "Can I take Prescott with me?"

"Why do you want to do that?" replied his mom.

"I need him for protection." Lucas had no idea why he said that or why he would need protection.

His mom replied, playing along with what she thought was his imaginary game,

"Sure, if you think you need protection," she added. "I made the shoulder pack you asked for. It's

on the kitchen table. Please be careful and don't let him out of it."

Lucas thanked his mom with a kiss, grabbed the pack, and ran to get Prescott. As he was taking him out of the cage, Lucas asked, "Did you do that?"

"Of course I did. I told you we needed to do something important. Do you have the Power Ring?"

"It's in my pocket," replied Lucas.

"Good. We need to go now!"

Lucas was surprised at the urgency in Prescott's voice. He put Prescott in the shoulder pack and slipped it over his head. He walked quickly toward the bridge at the end of the court with Prescott riding in the pack across his chest. What Lucas did not know is that Kevin lived on the other side of the creek near the bridge. Kevin saw Lucas go down into the creek bed and, with a wicked grin, thought he would have some fun with Lucas.

Prescott was in Lucas's head again. *"After you get to the creek, get the ball and throw it back to your mom. Then we need to find the crystal for the ring."*

Lucas did as instructed. He soon found the ball and threw it back over the fence.

His mom yelled, "Thanks honey. See you back at the house."

"Lucas, now go to the bridge and look for a flat rectangular stone in the ground next to the cement wall," said Prescott. *"Under the stone you will find a small metal box and inside the box is the Fire Crystal."*

As Lucas went under the bridge, he did not see that he was being watched. Lucas located the stone by the wall, but the edges were covered with dirt. The stone was about the size of his mom's pancake griddle and almost as flat. With a stick he found

nearby, he dug the dirt away from the edges so he could grip the stone. He bent to lift it, but it wouldn't budge. "Whoa, this is heavy!" exclaimed Lucas. "I can't move it at all."

"Let me try," said Prescott.

In awe, Lucas watched as the stone slowly lifted and moved to the side to reveal a small golden box.

"Wow! How did you do that?" asked Lucas.

"Please hurry and open the box," urged Prescott. *"We do not have much time."*

Lucas reached into the cavity that was under the rectangular stone and removed the golden box. He sat on a nearby rock with the box on his lap and opened the lid to reveal a red crystal that was a little smaller than a dime.

"Now, hold the crystal over the center of the Power Ring, Lucas."

As he did, Lucas heard Prescott say something in a language he had never heard before and the crystal slipped from his fingers. It felt like it was being pulled into the ring with the force of a strong magnet. The Power Ring started vibrating and getting warmer.

"Turn the outer ring so that the arrow is pointing to the symbol that is a Double-S," said Prescott, with some urgency in his voice. *"Squeeze the crystal now! Someone is coming. You need to trust me now,"* added Prescott, *"Be very still and I promise you will be invisible to anyone who might be looking for you."*

He did exactly as Prescott had instructed and wondered who would be looking for him under the bridge. A few seconds later, Lucas saw a small landslide of rocks and dirt and heard someone coming down the bank to the creek. He groaned to himself when he saw Kevin Cherno come around the corner of the cement wall with a plastic bag. As Lucas held his breath, his heart started pounding. He bent over a little as if he could hide by making himself a little smaller.

Lucas heard Prescott say, "*So this is the Kevin in your class? You do not need to fear. To him you are invisible.*"

Lucas was still scared. He looked behind him to see if he could run that way, but his escape was blocked by overgrown bushes. He could make a run for it across the creek, but he would get his shoes and pants wet. There was no going forward since Kevin was blocking any escape in that direction. Lucas decided that he would just have to trust Prescott, so he sat very still.

Kevin was scanning the area under the bridge looking for rocks that Lucas may have hidden behind.

"Hey Lucas," Kevin called out taunting him. "Come on out, I have a surprise for you."

"*Lucas,*" said Prescott in a very soft and calm voice, clearly feeling Lucas's fear, "*even though you can see yourself, Kevin cannot see us.*"

Sure enough, Kevin looked *directly* at Lucas but did not show any signs of recognition!

"Lucas, I know you are down here," said Kevin teasingly. "I saw you come down to get your ball. Come out, come out, wherever you are."

Lucas sat very still as Kevin walked closer to where he and Prescott were sitting. His heart was pounding so hard he could now hear the thumping in his own ears. Kevin came within about ten feet of where Lucas was sitting on the rock as he continued to look for places where he thought Lucas might be hiding.

He heard Kevin mumble, "I guess that little twerp slipped out the other side. Too bad he's going to miss the surprise I had for him."

Kevin reached into the plastic bag and pulled out a water balloon and threw it against the cement wall across the creek. It hit the wall and burst with a splash. He pulled out another and threw it at the rock Lucas was sitting on. Just before Lucas closed his eyes, expecting to get wet, he saw the balloon swerve and hit the ground beside the rock. Kevin had a puzzled look on his face as he wondered how the balloon curved and missed the rock.

"That is how the power of telekinesis works my young friend," said Prescott.

Lucas smiled and silently said to Prescott, *"That's just too cool!"*

Kevin pulled out another balloon and with determination, aimed directly at the same rock and the unseen Lucas. He threw the balloon, but to his surprise, the water balloon didn't pop. Instead, it bounced off an *invisible wall*, came right back at Kevin and broke against his belt buckle, soaking him from the waist down.

"Hey!" Kevin howled. "What the heck! How is that possible? It should have broken on the rock!"

Angrily, Kevin pulled out the last balloon and just as he was throwing it overhand, he squeezed so hard that the balloon exploded above his head drenching him.

"Aaahh!" screamed Kevin as he angrily kicked the dirt.

Lucas could not help himself from giggling out loud. Kevin spun around and looked right in Lucas's direction. Lucas froze, but Kevin made no movement toward him. Finally, Kevin turned and started to climb back up the bank, but instead, turned toward the creek. He began to cross the creek by stepping on the rocks sticking out of the water. Half way across, Kevin stepped on a rock that rolled downward and so did he, falling in about a foot of water. He screamed and splashed in frustration. Kevin stood up, soggy and dripping wet, and splashed as he walked the next few feet to the bank on the other side of the creek. When he finally disappeared around the corner of the bridge, Lucas allowed himself to laugh out loud.

"Prescott? Did you move that rock in the creek?"

"No, Kevin did that all by himself."

FIVE

Power to Choose

Destiny is not subject to chance,
but fashioned by the choices we make.

Lucas held Prescott in one hand and with the other put the golden box in the bottom of the shoulder pack. Then he gently placed Prescott on top of the box. As he walked up the creek bank he looked at the Power Ring with the crystal now firmly affixed in the center of the ring and wondered about using the Power Ring on Kevin.

"I thought the Power Ring was to be used for good. Getting Kevin wet with the balloons wasn't good, was it?" asked Lucas.

Prescott replied, *"The Power Ring is to be used for good, but it can be used as a protection against*

those who would attack and harm you. It would be good if both you and Kevin can learn something from today's adventure."

As he thought about what happened, Lucas said, "My dad always says, 'what goes around, comes around.' Maybe Kevin learned that he will be treated just like he treats others."

"*Sometimes what goes around does not come as quickly as it did for Kevin today, but trust me, it always comes around,*" said Prescott. "*What about you? What did you learn?*"

Lucas thought for a moment, "I suppose I learned I could trust you."

Lucas was surprised to hear the chameleon laugh and say, "*That would be a great lesson to learn!*"

Lucas thought hard about what else he learned. "How about actions have consequences."

"*Excellent!*" said Prescott. "*We can make a choice, but we do not get to choose the consequence. There are some laws that cannot be broken. For example, if someone makes the choice to jump off of a cliff and then changes their mind, they must still obey the law of gravity. Unless they have wings to fly, they will still fall. You see, the consequence is connected directly to the choice. People make choices all the time and then try to blame others for the bad consequences that follow. What they do not understand is that we do not get to choose the consequence after we make the choice.*

"You need to get home now. Besides, I am ready for some more crickets."

When Lucas got home, his mother asked, "What took you so long? Is everything all right?"

Lucas replied, "Everything is fine. I just stopped to look at some rocks under the bridge."

"Well, now that you are home, I need your help with a few things around the house. Will you please put away your toys? They're scattered throughout the family room—and put your books on the shelves in your bookcase. But first, I need you to sweep the leaves and grass off of the walkway and front porch. I have some friends coming over in about thirty minutes, honey, and I don't want the leaves or grass clippings tracked into the house."

"Okay Mom," said Lucas cheerfully. Lucas put Prescott in his comfy cage and he went to the garage to get the broom. Lucas wondered if he could use the Power Ring to move the grass away from the porch toward the sidewalk. It would be much faster than sweeping! As Lucas stood on the porch, he turned the pointer on the ring to the Three Arrows, squeezed the crystal and thought about the grass moving toward the street.

What happened next was a total surprise! Instead of moving away from the house, the leaves and grass clippings swirled up from the ground into a miniature whirlwind. This "grassy tornado" flew around the lawn picking up more loose grass and leaves, getting bigger and bigger!

"Cool," said Lucas. But then, all of a sudden, the swirling leaves and grass came right towards him and the porch!

"No, no, no!" yelled Lucas, and then he remembered the ring and released his hold on it,

and the grass and leaves just dropped to the ground, in the middle of the walkway.

Lucas heard Prescott's voice in his head,

"Are you having a little trouble sweeping the porch?"

Lucas was not sure if Prescott was asking a simple question or if there was a hint of amusement in his voice.

"What I am doing wrong?" asked Lucas.

"Lucas, who were you helping? You or your mother?"

"Well, I was helping my mother." said Lucas.

"True, you are helping your mother, but you are also trying to take a shortcut. Work is very important to building character and there are no shortcuts to character building."

"Then using the ring to clean my room would probably not work either," sighed Lucas.

"I thought that might be coming next. No, you need to clean your room with your hands the way normal boys clean their rooms."

"All right! I'll get the broom and sweep the normal way like everybody else," said Lucas glumly and wondered if magic could ever be just for fun.

Lucas had just finished sweeping up all of the grass when the first guest pulled up in front of the house. He quickly went inside to pick up his things from the family room. Lucas released a few crickets into Prescott's cage and heard Prescott say, "*Ahh, dinner! Thank you!*"

"*Lucas, I need to tell you something very important. You will be tempted to use the ring to help others, and that is good—as long as you do not do anything that will affect the course of history.*"

Lucas asked, "But how will I know if my choice affects history?"

"*You will need to follow your heart and listen very closely to what your heart tells you.*"

"Oh, you mean like listening to my conscience?" asked Lucas.

"*Yes, it is like listening to your conscience, but it is more than that.*" said Prescott. "*This gift you are developing will speak to your mind, but you will feel it in your heart. As you develop your gift and it becomes stronger, you will wonder how you can use this gift in other ways. Your heart will tell you. For example, when you thought about using the ring to clean your room, what did your heart tell you?*"

"It told me that maybe I was cheating," said Lucas. "But Prescott, sometimes it feels like *you* are my conscience."

"*I suppose it might feel that way to you, but your heart will take over that job. It is my responsibility, however, to teach you and to help you become the best you can be.*"

"What do you mean it's your responsibility to teach me? Did someone tell you to do that?" asked Lucas.

"*I have been teaching young students like you for many years. As one who has mastered the skills of the Power Ring, I have the responsibility to teach others who are worthy and deserve these powers. You want to learn to master the ring, yes? Well, by learning to master the Power Ring, you will also be learning to master yourself.*"

Lucas knew Prescott was a lot older than he and definitely wiser. He also realized that Prescott had chosen him for a reason. He *did* want to learn more about himself and understand the reason he was chosen. He wanted to master the Power Ring and have the adventures that could come with it.

"I want to learn everything you can teach me," Lucas declared firmly.

"*Lucas, the choices we make are dependent on the knowledge we have. The more we know and understand, the better our choices can be. Knowledge is the key to success. Along with the knowledge and power that comes with the ring, you have the responsibility to learn all you can.*"

"Do you mean learn all I can in school?" asked Lucas.

"*There is much you will learn in school, but you can also learn by observing and reading. Lucas, do you know the difference between knowledge and wisdom?"*

Lucas thought about this for a moment and replied, "Knowledge is what you know in your head and wisdom is…" Lucas hesitated to see if his heart would give him the answer as Prescott had promised, and then it came to him. "Knowledge is what you know in your head and wisdom is how you use that knowledge with your heart."

"That is absolutely correct! Now, how about some more crickets?"

SIX

Frozen in Time

> After everyone is gone, make sure
> you like the person left behind.

Now that the Fire Crystal was part of the Power Ring, Lucas hoped it was time to start learning how to use its power.

"Lucas, before you begin your training in the different elements of the Power Ring, I would like you to look up the meaning of your name," said Prescott.

"Do you mean Lucas or Lightfoot?" asked Lucas.

"Both names," replied Prescott. *"I think you will find that the meaning of your names can have significance in your life."*

After he released some crickets into Prescott's cage, Lucas went to the family room computer and looked up his name on the Internet. He discovered that "Lucas" meant light in several languages. He also read that "Lightfoot" had its origins in England and it was the name of someone who was a speedy runner or messenger. He wondered if that meant that he was a messenger of light. Maybe it had something to do with the symbol on the ring that looked like the sun.

Lucas then heard Prescott in his mind and realized Prescott was listening in on his thoughts. *"Yes, Lucas, it has everything to do with the Light Power symbol. If you are patient, when the time is right, I will teach you everything you need to know about the Light Power."*

Lucas was excited to learn how to use the all of the powers behind the symbols on the Power Ring. He figured that being patient must be a super power that he had yet to learn.

That night after dinner, Lucas carried Prescott into the backyard so Lucas could practice some of the things he had been taught. He pulled the Power Ring from his pocket and turned the pointer to the Three Arrows for telekinesis and squeezed the crystal.

Prescott said, *"Look at an object and think about where you want it to be."*

Lucas was sitting on the tire swing and looked at a plastic sand bucket sitting outside the sandbox. He began to imagine the bucket inside the sandbox and to his amazement the bucket actually started moving! Lucas got so excited that he lost his concentration and the bucket banged into the side of the sandbox.

"Wow! Did you see that? That was so cool!" exclaimed Lucas.

"*Yes, Lucas, that was cool,*" chuckled Prescott. "*Now try it again. This time concentrate on putting the bucket inside the sandbox.*"

Lucas tried a few more times until he was successful.

"*Very good,*" said Prescott. "*Now try something a little larger.*"

Lucas noticed that the wooden steps up to the trampoline had fallen over. He concentrated on lifting the steps back into place and was able to move them upright after only dropping them a few times.

"*Excellent,*" said Prescott. "*Now I would like you to practice moving many things at once. There are many pine needles on the trampoline, but they are light. I want you to move all of them at once. Do not think of them as many objects, but just one. Move them as if there was a gust of wind.*"

Lucas concentrated a little longer and a little harder, and within a few moments all of the needles blew off the trampoline as if they were all glued together.

Prescott asked, *"How did you do that so quickly?"*

"Well," said Lucas, "I took your idea, but instead of moving the needles, I thought about moving the air across the surface so that the wind would do the work."

"You are indeed a fast learner," said Prescott. *"You have learned to use the elements around you to accomplish your goal. Remember what you have learned this day. The time will come when you will need to use the things that you find in nature for your safety."*

Lucas asked, "Can I practice being invisible?"

Prescott agreed, and Lucas turned the pointer to the Double-S and squeezed the crystal. He felt the ring vibrate slightly and he realized he didn't know what to do next. Then he heard Prescott in his mind.

"Imagine that there is a curtain between you and everyone else all around you."

There was no one else in the backyard so he just imagined a curtain surrounding him and that his little brother was coming out of the back door. To his amazement, the screen door opened and his brother Gavin stepped out and yelled, "Lucas! Mom wants you to come in!"

Gavin saw the tire swing moving and thought that Lucas must have just gotten off, so he came closer to look around the side of the house. Lucas was still on the swing as Gavin walked by but he didn't see Lucas. Gavin called out again, with no response, so he went back into the house.

Lucas let go of the ring, put it back into his pocket, picked up Prescott and began walking to the house. Just as he got to the screen door, his mom opened it.

"Oh, there you are! Gavin said he couldn't find you," exclaimed his mom.

"I was hiding and pretending I was invisible," said Lucas, "but I came when I heard him call me." His mom just shook her head as Lucas came into the house.

It had been another eventful day and Lucas had learned much from Prescott. He was glad it was Friday and he would not have to see Kevin until Monday at school. The next two days Lucas practiced the things he had learned from Prescott. Lucas was determined that he was never going to let Kevin scare him again.

☼ ☼ ☼

On Saturday morning, Lucas asked if he could ride his bike over to his cousin's house a few streets away. His mom agreed, but he was to have Aunt Lisa call her when he got there. Lucas decided to take the shortcut to his cousin's house, which was across the footpath bridge where he had encountered Kevin earlier. He didn't expect to see Kevin, but he was wrong.

As Lucas rode up to the bridge, he saw Kevin on the other side tossing a Frisbee to his dog. Kevin must live in the house nearest to the bridge. Lucas thought about going the long way around to his cousin's house, but remembered his resolve not to be afraid of Kevin. Prescott had taught Lucas how to use the Power Ring for stopping time, so Lucas turned the pointer to the Double-T with the circle and held it in his hand.

As Lucas rode his bike over the bridge, he squeezed the crystal. Kevin's back was to Lucas and he had just thrown the Frisbee. The dog was in midair, about to bite down on the Frisbee, when everything stopped moving...except Lucas. Kevin

froze with his arm stretched out, amazingly his dog froze in midair, and everything got very quiet. It was so quiet that Lucas could not even hear the wind in his ears.

Lucas rode by on the sidewalk several feet from where Kevin was standing like a statue in jeans and a t-shirt. When he was far enough down the street, Lucas stopped, turned around, and looked back at Kevin as he let go of the crystal in the ring. It was funny to see Kevin and his dog frozen in time and then to see them moving again—just as if nothing had happened! Lucas smiled all the way to his cousin's house.

SEVEN

Bully-Bending

*That which you send into the life of others
will come back into your own.*

Kevin Cherno had moved to the area about two
years earlier and quickly made a reputation for
himself at school. He would be sneaky and do
things to the other students that he could easily
deny, and then make sure they saw him grinning
as they discovered what he had done. Last month
Kevin let the air out of Lucas's bike tires and he had
to walk his bike home. Kevin rode past and said,
"What's the matter, Lucas? Feeling a little deflated?"
And then he laughed. It was the mean way he was
laughing that confirmed to Lucas that Kevin was the
one who had done it.

Lucas felt a combination of apprehension and excitement as he got ready for school on Monday morning. He remembered the fear he'd felt under the bridge as Kevin was looking for him. He also remembered something that Prescott had told him on the walk back from the creek.

"When you fear someone, one way to change that feeling is to imagine that person with big mouse ears, a long mouse tail and a squeaky mouse voice. And then in your mind, shrink them down to the size of a small gray mouse."

Lucas began smiling as he thought about Kevin. Lucas made a black and white picture in his mind of a miniature Kevin with big mouse ears, a mouse tail and a high-pitched voice. Lucas practiced this several times over the weekend, and again as he was going to school. This time he felt a little less nervous about seeing Kevin at school.

When Lucas got to his classroom, he sat down next to Hailey and said, "Hey!"

She smiled back, "Hi, Lucas, how was your weekend?"

Lucas thought about all of the excitement and the things that he had done with Prescott and the Power Ring, but remembering his promise, he just replied, "It was good."

He looked past Hailey as Kevin sat down. Kevin looked over at Lucas and gave him an angry stare. Lucas started feeling the same fear he had felt at the creek and then remembered what Prescott had taught him and he started to laugh as he looked away from Kevin and down at his desk.

Hailey asked him, "What are you laughing about?"

"Oh, it's nothing. I was just imagining some big mouse ears," said Lucas grinning.

The bell rang and Miss Harrison stood up. "Good morning class. It's time to share your homework assignment." There were a few audible groans.

Lucas's class had been studying poetry, and Miss Harrison had given the assignment to the class to write a poem about something that had special meaning in their lives. There were quite a variety of topics from the students. Hailey had written about friends, Kevin had a short poem about his dog, and Sarah read her poem about spending time at the beach with her family. When it came time for Lucas, he went to the front of the class and said:

"I met a new friend in my neighborhood and he has taught me some very important lessons. This poem is about one of those lessons. The name of my poem is *The Boomerang*."

Life is like a boomerang,
I know that this is true.
What you send to the lives of others,
Will always come back to you.

It matters not how far it flies,
Or how long its curve.
For surely as the sun comes up,
It'll return what you deserve.

Listen closely to this advice,
It's what we all must do.
Send out friendship, words of kindness,
And they will come back to you.

Lucas had meant this poem mostly for Kevin, but Miss Harrison said that it was a good reminder of the Golden Rule.

At the beginning of lunch, Lucas was walking by as Kevin was getting a drink at the drinking fountain. Kevin looked up, ran his hand through the stream of water and splashed water on Lucas.

"I missed you at the creek," said Kevin.

"What do you mean?" questioned Lucas.

"I saw you go down to the creek," said Kevin, "but then you disappeared."

"I disappeared? That sounds like magic," said Lucas with a smile.

He could see that Kevin was getting mad and thought that maybe he needed to cool off. Kevin was standing in front of the drinking with his hand still on the handle and the water still flowing. Lucas remembered what Prescott had taught him about stopping time, and using his mind, Lucas turned the pointer on the Power Ring in his pocket to the Double-T symbol and imagined squeezing the crystal. Everyone around Lucas slowed to a stop and the school corridor filled with kids became quiet. Lucas could hear nothing.

Lucas walked up to Kevin who was facing the drinking fountain. The water was still on, but motionless in a prefect arc. He helped Kevin bend over so his head leaned down toward the water fountain with his mouth in the stream of water. Lucas walked to the corner of the building and thought, *"What goes around comes around."*

Lucas let go of the crystal, and the weight of Kevin's hand kept the water flowing, soaking his head! He heard Kevin yelp and could see the surprised look on Kevin's face as he was getting his head drenched! Lucas was hoping that Kevin would learn that choosing to treat others unkindly was just like a boomerang.

EIGHT

The Book Bully

You cannot change a bully by being a bully.
Choose compassion over fear.

Miss Harrison took the class to the library every Wednesday to return books and to check out new books to read. This was the first time that Lucas could remember that the librarian, Mrs. Sanchez, was not at her desk to greet the students as they came in. Sitting in her chair was an unfamiliar lady greeting the class.

"Good morning Miss Harrison and welcome students," said the new librarian. "My name is Miss Miller and I am helping in the library today. Mrs. Sanchez and I have selected some books we thought might interest you. You will find them on the tables or you can look on the shelves for another book you'd like to read."

Miss Harrison thanked her and directed the students to look through the books that were spread out on top of the tables. As the students were walking around looking at the different books, Lucas saw Kevin grab a book out of Carlos's hands and told him to find another book. It was too bad Kevin was still being a bully. Most of the time, the kids Kevin picked on just let it go because they didn't want to cause a problem or become the focus of Kevin's attention. Lucas thought maybe he could use a little magic to help Carlos and also teach Kevin a lesson. Kevin pulled out a chair and started to sit down with a self-satisfied look on his face. Lucas thought about moving the chair so Kevin would fall on the floor when he sat down, but that was something a bully would do. Lucas did not want to be a bully like Kevin. Lucas had a better idea. Kevin was looking at the picture on the front cover of the book when Lucas walked over to him.

"Hey Kevin," said Lucas, "What's your book about?"

"Why do you care, Stinkyfoot?" asked Kevin angrily.

"I saw the cover had a picture of an alien creature and it just looked interesting," replied Lucas.

Kevin gave Lucas an irritated look and said, "The author's name is Kevin so the book has to be good. Besides, I like graphic novels."

"Cool! Enjoy the book," said Lucas.

Lucas turned to find a chair at another table and hid his smile. He thought that if he could use the power of telekinesis to move things, then he might be able to use the same power to stop something from moving. He found a chair next to Hailey that was two tables away from Kevin. As he sat down on his chair, Lucas turned the pointer on the Power Ring with his mind to the Three Arrows. He squeezed the crystal and imagined Kevin's book closed. Then he held up his own book so he could look over the top of it at Kevin and the book he was holding.

Kevin went to open the book, but the front and back cover refused to open. He put the book down in his lap to get a better grip and using his finger tips he tried again to open the book, but still it would not open. Grunting, he turned the book over several times to look at the edges to see if there was a latch. Kevin looked up from the book and glanced around to see if anyone was watching him. Lucas quickly dropped his head down and looking down at his own book, pretended he had not seen anything. He found it difficult not to smile. In frustration, Kevin slid the book across the table hard enough to hit the book that Carlos was reading.

"Here you go," said Kevin. "I decided I don't want to read this book after all."

Carlos was surprised and eyed Kevin cautiously as he took the book.

Kevin crossed his arms and sat staring at Carlos. Kevin was getting ready to laugh at Carlos as he tried to open the book. Lucas released the crystal on the Power Ring and watched Kevin. Hailey looked up at that moment and noticed that Lucas was not reading, but looking across the room at the table where Kevin and Carlos were sitting.

"What's going on?" asked Hailey.

"I'm not sure," whispered Lucas, "but I think Kevin is being a bully again and this time it might backfire on him."

Carlos put his own book down. He picked up the graphic novel and opened the book with ease.

Kevin stared at the open book and clamped his teeth in anger. "I changed my mind. Give me back that book!"

Carlos knew that voice. Kevin used it whenever he bullied someone. Carlos closed the book and slid it across the table back to Kevin. By this time, the other students at Kevin's table were watching with curiosity. With his mind, Lucas squeezed the crystal on the Power Ring to hold the book closed. The other students at the table were watching Kevin, as once again, he tried to open the book without success. Kevin's face turned red and he looked like he was ready to explode as he slammed the book on the table! Carlos looked puzzled and wondered why Kevin was so angry. The other kids at the table looked at Kevin and sat back in their chairs in fear.

"What are you looking at?" said Kevin angrily as he jumped up, knocking his chair onto the floor with a loud bang and stormed out of the library.

As he turned to watch Kevin run out of the library, Lucas accidentally dropped his own book on the floor. Lucas was totally surprised to see Kevin look like he was ready to cry! Lucas never imagined that a bully like Kevin *could* cry. When he bent down to pick up his book he heard some of the students whispering to one another, trying to figure out what had just happened.

"Go back to your reading," said Miss Harrison as she got up and followed Kevin outside.

Hailey leaned over to Lucas and whispered, "What just happened?"

"Kevin was being a bully over a book he took from Carlos."

Just as he said that, Lucas heard a voice that sounded like his dad.

"Who is being the bully now?"

Lucas looked around the room expecting to see his dad, but the only adult in the library was Miss Miller. A minute later, Miss Harrison came back inside the library and asked Carlos to come with her.

"Oh, no! Someone's in trouble," whispered Hailey to Lucas. "What do you think Kevin did to Carlos? Or did Carlos do something to Kevin?"

"Maybe someone else did something to Kevin," suggested Lucas in a whisper.

"Really? Who?" asked Hailey.

Lucas shrugged his shoulders, but inside he knew. He was starting to regret what he had done, which made him realize that his actions could not be undone. Hailey went back to reading her book and Lucas looked at the book he had picked up and put back on the table. He thought he should go back to reading his book, but the truth was, he had not read anything. He suddenly realized that *he* was the cause of the disturbance in what was supposed to be a quiet library! He thought about what the voice had said. He *was* being a bully, but just in a different way. Maybe reading would take his mind off of his mistake.

Lucas was surprised when he couldn't open his own book! It was clamped shut just like Kevin's book! At that moment, he remembered Prescott saying that the Power Ring can only be used for good and unselfish reasons. Using the Power Ring on Kevin had backfired. Lucas quickly felt annoyed that he couldn't open the book. He felt even more annoyed that he couldn't use the Power Ring to help others. He told himself he *was* helping Carlos. That's when Lucas heard the voice again.

"How did you help Carlos?"

The voice wasn't in his mind like Prescott but it wasn't quite audible in his ears either. Lucas looked around to see where the voice was coming from. He started to ask Hailey if she had heard anything, but she was concentrating on her own book.

Something did not feel right. Lucas felt like someone was watching him. He turned to his right and saw Miss Miller looking at him, and she was not smiling. In fact, she had a strange look on her face. Lucas turned back to the book that would not open. Like a magnet, his eyes were pulled back to the substitute librarian. This time she motioned for him to come over to the desk.

Lucas now knew that he may have used his power unwisely, but he told himself not to worry. The librarian didn't know what he had done. He told himself that he had used the power for good to help Carlos and all the kids who were afraid of Kevin. Because he had the power, Lucas thought it was his responsibility to teach Kevin that being a bully has consequences. But Lucas now thought that using the Power Ring had led to consequences beyond what he had expected. He walked up to the desk and stood in front of Miss Miller.

"I have already introduced myself to the class. What's your name?" asked Miss Miller.

"Lucas Lightfoot," he replied

"Well Lucas, I was watching everyone in the room," said Miss Miller in a low voice. "I wonder what is going on with the two boys in your class. Don't they get along?"

"Kevin, the tall boy, has trouble getting along with almost everybody," said Lucas.

"Does it seem strange to you that Kevin could not open the book?" asked Miss Miller quietly. "And yet, I saw Carlos opened the book without a problem."

She really did see everything! Now Lucas was feeling even more uncomfortable and guilty for playing a trick on Kevin.

"I was watching the boys to see if there was going to be a problem," said Miss Miller. "And I was watching you. Lucas, you were the only one smiling as you watched what was going on between Kevin and Carlos."

"Was I smiling?" asked Lucas.

"Yes, you were. I see things that most people do not see," whispered Miss Miller. "What I saw today was someone who was taking pleasure in another person's misfortune."

Her comment surprised Lucas because he was not that kind of person. But today, he knew she was right as he struggled to sort out his feelings. He felt guilty for what he had done to Kevin and sad for the way it affected him. He had been given power, but he realized that he had a lot to learn in how to use that power wisely.

Lucas wondered if the librarian knew what had really happened. Did Miss Miller know about the Power Ring and what he was able to do with it? He was certainly not about to say anything to give away the secret he had with Prescott. But Lucas realized that even though he may have had good intentions, he was being a bully toward Kevin and had forgotten to follow his heart.

Miss Miller dispelled the sadness Lucas was feeling with a wave of her hand and for a moment he felt like a burden had been lifted.

"Come around the desk," she whispered. "I have a special book for you. This book came in today and I think you will enjoy reading it."

Lucas was curious and walked around the desk to where Miss Miller was sitting. She opened a drawer and pulled out an old book. The book was about five inches wide and eight inches tall and maybe a half-inch thick. The book was covered with dark brown polished leather and had a design carved into the front cover. The pattern on the leather reminded him of some of the belts he had seen at the county fair where a belt maker was working with his tools to create an image in the leather.

"I think this book will interest you," said Miss Miller with a smile.

"What's it about?" asked Lucas.

She handed the book to Lucas. It had a fancy design carved into the leather and at the bottom he saw his name, "LIGHTFOOT," engraved into the leather.

In a low voice, Miss Miller said, "This book is about the Lightfoot family that sailed over from England many years ago. You might discover things in these pages that will help you."

"What sort of things?" asked Lucas.

"I don't know what you will find," said Miss Miller. "That's up to you. The importance of this book or any book is the meaning it has for you. Keep the book as long as you like. This book does not belong to the library and does not need to be returned. Just think of it as a gift to you and your family."

"Who gave you this book? Where did it come from?" asked Lucas.

"The giver wishes to remain nameless," said Miss Miller. "I was only asked to give you this book and to tell you to search through the pages to help you find your answers."

This was sounding like some of the conversations he had with Prescott and Lucas wondered if Miss Miller was more that just a substitute librarian!

"But what are my questions?"

"Again, that's up to you Lucas," said Miss Miller. "There are many books you will read that seem to be just a simple story. But hidden in the book is another story that can be understood only when you imagine yourself as a character in the story. If you ask questions about the meaning behind the words and the story, the answers will be revealed."

Sometimes Lucas was bothered when adults didn't answer the question or they answered a question with another question. Lucas realized that Miss Miller, just like Prescott, was not going to tell him what he wanted to know and he would have to do as she suggested. At that moment, Lucas had a brief picture flash in his mind. It was the memory of standing on the porch talking with Katrina and seeing the glow in her face. Lucas thought he could see the same glow in Miss Miller's face. He wondered if she knew about the Power Ring but was allowing him to keep it a secret.

Lucas heard the library door open and he looked over his shoulder to see Miss Harrison coming into the library.

"Okay class, library time is over," announced Miss Harrison. "Let's go back to our classroom."

Lucas turned back to the librarian to ask another question but, to his amazement, she was not there! He looked around the library for her, but Miss Miller had disappeared. There was no place for her to go—and yet she was gone.

Lucas waited for most of the kids to leave before he went back to the table where he was sitting. He picked up his other book and checked to see if it would open. It did. He used it to cover the book he had been given by the librarian. Lucas followed the students back to the classroom and when he got to his desk he put the Lightfoot Family book into his backpack and sat down.

Miss Miller had given him something to think about. The voice he heard, whomever it was, had also given him reason to think about his actions. Lucas looked at Kevin's empty chair and wondered if his own actions were any different from Kevin's. He couldn't stop thinking about what he had done in the library. Despite his good intentions, *he* was being a bully to Kevin. Lucas knew he had misused the Power Ring and that was probably the reason he was feeling so bad.

Hailey also saw that Kevin's seat was empty. She leaned over to Lucas and asked, "What happened to Kevin?"

"I don't know," whispered Lucas. It was an unwritten rule that when someone was in trouble at school, it was best not to ask but to wait for the teacher to explain it to the class. That did not stop the students from guessing what happened or making up wild stories about the person in trouble. Miss Harrison was always good about helping the students learn from the experiences of others.

"Class, there was a bit of trouble in the library today," said Miss Harrison. "Someone was playing a joke on Kevin and you all saw that he got angry.

He and I had a chat and he has calmed down. Kevin thought Carlos was responsible, but after talking with both boys, I have reason to believe it was someone else. Kevin will be back at school tomorrow and there will be no talk of what happened today. I'm sure the person responsible for playing a joke on Kevin will consider the consequences of his or her actions and will not repeat them."

Lucas did not feel good being a bully and he promised himself he would never do that again!

NINE

History Mystery

*The painful lessons are often the ones
that have the greatest influence in our lives.*

After lunch, when they were back inside the classroom, Hailey turned to Lucas and asked, "What's wrong?"

"What makes you think anything is wrong?"

"It's that thing you do with your hands," replied Hailey. "You tap your fingers on your legs."

Lucas started to protest when he realized he was doing exactly that. He put the palms of his hands on his pants to wipe off the sweat.

"Well, all I can say is, I think I need to change how I treat other people," said Lucas.

"What's wrong with the way you treat people?"

"I was laughing on the inside at Kevin in the library. Even though he may be a bully, he's still a person with feelings," said Lucas. He still felt bad for what he had done.

Hailey was surprised to see Lucas so serious and said, "You were not the only one laughing at Kevin. The whole class knows he's a bully, and when something happens to him, maybe he's just getting what he deserves."

"Maybe so." replied Lucas. "It's kind of weird, but I feel embarrassed for him."

Hailey liked Lucas. He was different from the other boys in the class. He was usually happy and sometimes funny. She could now add serious and sensitive to his character traits. Hailey would write more about Lucas in her journal when she got home. In fact, most of what she had written lately had been about Lucas.

☼ ☼ ☼

Lucas was anxious to see what was in the Lightfoot Family book. The sound of the bell signaling the end of school put Lucas on his feet. He said a quick goodbye to Hailey and headed for the door. He felt the added weight of the book given to him by the librarian. There was something about the book that tugged at him. He felt drawn to read about the past in order to learn about his future.

When Lucas got home, the sweet smell of freshly baked cookies filled the house and Lucas hoped some chocolate chip cookies were in his future.

"Hi Honey! How was school today?" asked his mom.

"Oh, you know. Like every other day," replied Lucas. "Can I have some cookies?"

Lucas's mom scooped up a couple of warm cookies from the tray and placed them on a napkin.

"Thanks! Can I eat them at my desk?" asked Lucas. "I want to get started on my homework."

"Yes, but don't make a mess," replied his mom.

"I'm not the messy one, that's Gavin," said Lucas with a grin as he headed for his bedroom. He needed to talk with Prescott about the librarian at school. Lucas set the napkin on his desk and took the new book from his backpack and dropped it onto the desk next to Prescott's cage.

"Hey, Prescott," said Lucas. "Something happened today at school and I need to talk with you."

"Hello, Lucas. You sound concerned. I hope your day was good," replied Prescott.

"Well, there was certainly some excitement in the library."

Lucas explained to Prescott what he had done to try to teach Kevin a lesson, how it backfired on him and how badly he felt afterward. He told Prescott about the substitute librarian and about the Lightfoot Family book she had given him.

"Prescott, what seemed really strange is that I think the librarian, Miss Miller, *knew* I had used the Power Ring. Does she know about the Power Ring?" asked Lucas.

Prescott turned to face Lucas and looked directly at him to show Lucas he was giving him his full attention.

"Why was I given this power if I can't use it to help others?" asked Lucas in frustration.

"That is exactly why you were given the Power Ring," replied Prescott. *"You must use this special power to help others, but your responsibility is to learn how and when."*

"I really blew it today with Kevin," said Lucas. "Sometimes I wish you were with me to tell me what to do so I don't mess up."

"Lucas, I cannot make your decisions. I can guide you, but you must decide how and when to use your power. You will make mistakes and you will not always choose wisely, but that is how you learn. Lucas, there will be people coming into your life who will be watching you and helping you. You have been given a great responsibility and a great power that comes with the Power Ring. You used your power poorly today. I believe

the lesson was not for Kevin, but it was meant for you."

"I think you're right," said Lucas. "I didn't look ahead to think about the consequences of my actions. You don't need to worry about me making that mistake again!"

"That is good to hear," replied Prescott. *"The painful lessons are often the ones that have the greatest influence in our lives."*

Sometimes Lucas felt like Prescott knew everything that was going on his life but allowed events to unfold as they did, so Lucas could have the experience. He now knew why Prescott didn't warn him when he was getting ready to make a mistake. He would have to rely on his head and his heart.

Lucas thought that the gift of the book was a little strange. In fact, most of the strange things that happened to him recently were somehow related to Prescott coming into his life. Lucas hoped Prescott might know something about the Lightfoot Family book.

"Do you know why I was given this book?" asked Lucas as he pointed to it on his desk.

"It appears that this book is about the history of the Lightfoot family," replied Prescott. *"I suppose you will be able to learn something about the people in the book. But my guess*

is you were given the book to learn something about yourself."

That was just the kind of answer Lucas had come to expect from Prescott. There was enough information to get Lucas thinking but not enough to satisfy his desire to know. Lucas ran his fingers over the smooth leather cover with the LIGHTFOOT name engraved onto a scroll design. He opened the cover to read this message.

Dear reader: You hold in your hands the history of the Lightfoot family from England. The origin of our family name began as a nickname because our ancestors were quick messengers. Many members of the Lightfoot family have held important positions of responsibility throughout the history of England, Ireland and America as you will discover when you read the stories in these pages. If you are a descendant of the Lightfoot family, this story is yours. It is your story to understand from whence you began and where you can go as you write your own story.

Thomas Andrew Lightfoot 1882

On the next page Lucas saw a picture. It was the same image that was engraved into the leather on the book cover. He had seen something similar to this, but didn't know what they were called

until he read the words, "LIGHTFOOT COAT of ARMS". The coat of arms showed a heart on top of the helmet with a pin stuck in the heart. The shield had red and gold stripes with fancy ribbons around it. There was a black diagonal band adorned with three white shells on the shield. Under the coat of arms was a description:

The LIGHTFOOT COAT of ARMS granted to the Lightfoot Family in the Year of Our Lord 1394. The helmet represents wisdom, security and strength. The heart is the symbol for truth and sincerity. The pin in the heart represents passion. The shells symbolize protection and venture to foreign lands.

Captain John Lightfoot, Resident of Virginia, 1624.

Lucas turned the page and there was a portrait drawing of a man. It was as if the portrait was staring at Lucas. The caption under the picture read: Captain John Lightfoot, Resident of Virginia, 1624.

Lucas started to turn the page when he heard his dad.

"Lucas, what have you done with my name?"

Lucas turned around expecting to see his father standing in the doorway but he wasn't there. He looked at the clock and knew that his dad was not home from work yet. He looked over at Prescott who had his eyes closed and was warming himself under the light.

Again he heard the voice, *"Lucas, what have you done with my name?"*

As he looked at the picture of John Lightfoot, Lucas's jaw dropped open as he saw the picture of John Lightfoot begin moving—like in a movie!

"Lucas Lightfoot, what have you done with my name?"

Lucas quickly closed the book and slid it away from him.

"Prescott, did you hear that? The book was talking to me? Is this a magical book?"

"My young friend, it appears that the book about your ancestors is quite special," said Prescott. *"I believe your ancestors have taken an interest in you."*

"You must be joking! Why would dead people be interested in me?" asked Lucas. Immediately after asking, Lucas knew it was a silly question, because Prescott was serious and didn't joke. Lucas was beginning to accept that his life now was anything but normal and this must be a magical book. He wondered when he would get used to this "new normal" life.

"What do you think they want from me?"

"That may be a mystery that you need to solve. John Lightfoot has asked you a question. Maybe you should ask him what he wants from you," replied Prescott.

Lucas timidly pulled the book closer and carefully opened it to the page with the picture of John Lightfoot. Lucas was more careful with the book thinking that if he dropped it again, it would somehow hurt the people inside. He wondered if there were other pictures of ancestors and if they would also talk to him.

He felt kind of silly, but Lucas asked, "Captain Lightfoot, were you talking to me?"

When he answered Lucas, Captain John Lightfoot's image began to move like a movie again.

"Young Master Lucas, indeed I was speaking to you. I am Captain John Lightfoot, formally of Liverpool, England. I settled in Virginia and started a merchant business and a law practice. I am very interested in who you are. I believe all of your ancestors are concerned with whom you are becoming, young Lucas."

Lucas could not believe he was talking to a picture in a book! Not just any picture, but a moving picture that was talking back to him. But then again, at one time, he could not believe that a chameleon could talk with him either. The more he spoke, the more Lucas was amazed as the drawing of John Lightfoot transformed into a color movie.

"When I settled in Virginia, I built my business on honesty and helping others. I raised my sons to live the same way and they educated and trained their sons to follow the ideals that I lived by. Now, many

generations later, here you are. Lucas Lightfoot, you are my thirteenth great-grandson. So again I ask: What have you done with my name?"

"What do you mean?" asked Lucas.

"Your ancestors in the Lightfoot family have always carried their name with honor and pride," replied John Lightfoot. *"In my day, when a man said he would do something, then it was as good as done. A man's word was better than any contract written by a lawyer, even a lawyer as good as myself. The Lightfoot name has always been associated with integrity. I want you to consider how you honor the Lightfoot family name and how you are trusted by other people."*

"I try to be honest and do the right thing," said Lucas. "Sometimes I slip up, but I try to remember what my parents have taught me."

"What about the incident in the library today?" asked John Lightfoot.

"You saw that?" exclaimed Lucas.

"Of course I saw it. I was right there," declared his thirteenth great-grandfather.

"That was your voice I heard in the library," said Lucas excitedly. "You were the one who asked, 'Who is being the bully now?'"

"Yes, Master Lucas. I asked you that question so that you might think about your actions. How did it make you feel when you used the Lightfoot family name to trick a classmate?"

"Terrible!" replied Lucas as he hung his head down.

"Your friend Prescott has taught you a few things about the choices you make and the consequences that follow, has he not?" asked John Lightfoot.

"You know about Prescott?" asked Lucas, looking up quickly.

"My dear Master Lucas, I know more than you can imagine," said John Lightfoot in a soft voice. *"There have been others in the Lightfoot family that have been chosen and given the same power you now possess. Your grandfather, who bears my name, John Lightfoot, was also chosen."*

Lucas had never met his grandparents on his dad's side. They died before he was born. He had heard his dad talk about them and some of the adventures the family had growing up. Lucas thought about the picture of Grandma and Grandpa Lightfoot hanging in the hall and wished he could have met them. Lucas wondered if his Grandpa Lightfoot had been chosen, did he also have a Power Ring.

"You will soon discover why you were chosen and why you are so strong," said John Lightfoot.

"I don't feel very strong at all," said Lucas with a sigh.

"Strength is not always physical," said John Lightfoot. *"There are some people like you who have an inner strength. That strength does not make you better than anyone else, but rather always*

makes you better than you were. Because you have been chosen, more will be expected of you. You will have greater challenges, and like your Grandfather Lightfoot, you will have great adventures. I believe you will also have the strength to achieve greatness in your life."

"What if I don't want greatness? What if I want to be a kid again and forget about all of these strange magical things in my life?"

"You can choose a different path if that is what you want. But that is not what I see in your future," replied John Lightfoot.

"You can see my future?" asked Lucas.

As the moving picture of John Lightfoot began transforming back into a black and white drawing, his deep voice replied to Lucas. *"I can see your future because I have seen the past. What lies before you and what lies behind you are small matters to what lies within you. If I can help you become the person we all hope you will become, you know where to find me. I will be right here."*

Suddenly, Lucas heard his mom walking down the hall toward his room.

"Lucas, did I hear you talking to someone?" she asked.

"I was reading out loud from this book the substitute librarian at school gave me. She thought it would be fun for me to read about my ancestors," replied Lucas.

"Should I be worried about you, Lucas? You talk to a chameleon and now you are talking to ancestors in a book," teased Lucas's mom.

"Really Mom, I'm fine. There is nothing to worry about," replied Lucas.

"Well, let me know if your ancestors talk back to you," said his mom. "May I see the book?"

She picked up the book that was still open on the desk. He watched her reading the words silently and held his breath as she stared at the picture of Captain John Lightfoot. He fervently hoped that the picture would not start talking again!

At first, Lucas saw an expression of interest on his mom's face, but then it change to excitement as she stared at the picture.

"What's wrong Mom?"

"Come with me," she said, and Lucas followed her to the hallway where she had hung lots of old family pictures. She still had the book open as she was comparing the picture of Captain John Lightfoot to a picture on the wall.

"This picture of Captain John Lightfoot looks exactly like your Grandpa John Lightfoot when he was younger," observed his mom. "Where did you say you got this book?"

"From the school librarian," replied Lucas. "But she wasn't the regular librarian. She was substituting for Mrs. Sanchez. She said the book was a gift for us, but I don't know who it's from."

As his mom flipped through the pages, she said, "I am sure your father will want to see this. He has been researching his family history and this appears to be a treasure."

Lucas heard John Lightfoot in his thoughts saying, *"Lucas Lightfoot, this book will be a treasure in ways you cannot imagine!"*

"Oh, great!" thought Lucas. "Now I can hear my great-grandfather *and* Prescott in my head!"

Lucas wasn't sure if what he saw next really happened or if he just imagined it. Lucas *thought* he saw his Grandpa Lightfoot, whose picture was hanging on the wall, look down at the book in his mom's hands and then look directly at him—and wink!

TEN

Lunch Time Hero

Exercise your courage everyday. You might be surprised to know how much you have.

The next day at school, Lucas took his lunch to the far corner of the soccer field to be alone and to think. As he sat down on the cool grass, he thought about Prescott, the Power Ring and now he had a book of ancestors who talked with him. It all seemed like too much—and he just wanted to be a kid again. He felt like he was being pushed to have more responsibility than other boys his age. Did Captain John Lightfoot really see his future? What did he hope Lucas would become? Lucas felt a little reluctant as he was being drawn into a life that was so different from everyone else's. He liked the idea of having the Power Ring and being able to help other people, but it didn't work so well when he was trying to help Carlos in the library. Lucas was not sure if he wanted the responsibility that came with the Power Ring.

His troubled thoughts were interrupted when he heard a siren in the distance. That sound took him back several years to a time he and his dad drove to the foothills to see a wild fire. At first, Lucas thought it was kind of pretty to see the red glow on the hills at dusk. He had never seen the sun with such a deep red color. His dad had said it was because of all of the smoke in the air. All of a sudden, the wind shifted and the smoke and the fire started coming down the hill towards them. His dad was calm and started the truck to drive away, but Lucas was truly scared.

That night at home, Lucas had heard that his uncle, who was a fireman, was caught on a ridge with his fire crew. The wind had shifted on them and they were trapped with fire all around. They only had a few seconds to get into their fire shelters before the fire raced over them. One of the six-man crew did not survive. Lucas felt sad again as he thought about the funeral where he had seen the fireman's wife and children crying.

Every time he heard a siren from a fire truck, this memory came back to him and only intensified his fear of fire and being burned. The bell to end lunch brought him back to the present, and he started to walk to class.

Lucas spotted Hailey walking back from the outdoor lunch tables. She was looking down at the book she was reading. She was probably listening to music with the earphones she had in her ears. What she didn't see was a garbage truck backing up. She didn't hear the loud reverse beeping of the truck, and Lucas was sure she would not hear him yelling at her to stop. He had to act quickly. He immediately thought about the pointer on the ring, moved it to the Double-T and squeezed the crystal desperately. The shadow of the huge truck had just crossed Hailey's path when she looked up in horror. Everything slowed down and all movement came to a stop, except for Lucas. Hailey's book had fallen from her hands and was floating just above the ground. Her mouth was open in mid-scream and she was holding up her hands as if she could

stop the truck. Lucas ran over to Hailey, grabbed her book and her hand and pulled her to safety. They were up on the sidewalk out of the path of the truck when Lucas let go of the ring, the noise level increased, and the world around Lucas started moving again.

He was still holding Hailey's hand when she remembered the impending danger and felt her heart pounding. When she realized she was safe, she grabbed Lucas with both arms and gave him a hug of gratitude.

"Thank you!" she said. She was still shaking when she asked, "How did you do that? How did you save me from being run over by the trash truck?"

Lucas just smiled and said, "Sometimes we just react without thinking to save someone in danger. Besides, I just stopped time and moved you out of the way."

Lucas felt safe telling the truth because no one would believe he could actually stop time. Hailey figured he was just being funny. Yet, as she thought about what she could remember, she couldn't understand how it was possible for Lucas to do what he did. She was probably not going to get an answer she could believe or understand, so she said, "Well, however you did it, thank you very much."

"Hailey, can we keep this our secret? I don't want anyone to make a big deal out of this."

She saw how serious he was and replied, "Okay," as she gave his hand a squeeze. "It's our secret."

☼ ☼ ☼

That night at home, Lucas's mother got a phone call, but he did not pay attention to the conversation until he heard his mom say, "Yes, he's in Miss Harrison's class." Then he heard his mom say, "Well, that's not too surprising. Lucas has always been a helpful boy."

Lucas listened carefully to what his mother was saying. When he figured out it was Hailey's mom, Lucas thought, *"Oh great! Hailey told her mom!"*

His mom talked a little longer on the phone about school, teachers, children, and other things that didn't involve the garbage truck incident.

After she hung up, she came into Lucas's room and said, "Hailey Sinclair's mother called to thank you for saving Hailey's life."

"What did she tell you?" asked Lucas.

"She said that Hailey was about to step into a driveway with a garbage truck backing out and you stopped her. Is that what happened?" asked his mom.

"Yep, that's about right," replied Lucas.

He was glad that Hailey did not say exactly what happened, but then again, she wasn't too sure herself. Lucas liked being able to have a secret with Hailey.

ELEVEN

Hailey's Secret

*Secrets are often felt in the heart
before they are known in the mind.*

When Hailey got home from school, she greeted her mom, and then went to her room to write some thoughts and impressions in her journal. Her Siamese cat, Neko, was sunning himself on the window sill beside her bed. Hailey's dad had spent some time in Japan and started call her cat Neko, since that was the Japanese word for cat. Hailey liked it and the name stuck. The cat stood up and turned to look at Hailey as she sat on her bed.

"Hello, Neko. Did you have a lazy day sunning yourself or did you hunt for mice?"

Neko yawned, stretched his legs and jumped down to the bed where Hailey was sitting. After getting the mandatory scratching behind his ears, Neko curled up at the foot of the bed with all of the stuffed animals that Hailey kept there. Sometimes Neko would be asleep on Hailey's bed and blend in with the stuffed animals. Hailey opened her journal and began writing about the some of the things that had been on her mind.

I almost died yesterday! If it were not for the quick action of my friend Lucas, I would have been crushed by a garbage truck. But thanks to him, I am still alive. I still don't know how he did it. When he said he stopped time to save me, he sounded almost serious. But how is that possible? I know that Lucas is different from the other boys, but there is something really special about him. There is something strange about him, too. I think he has some secrets and I am going to find out what they are! He's funny, friendly, honest, and usually thoughtful. Over the last few days, I have seen a different side of Lucas. He can be serious. Most of the kids at school don't like Kevin Cherno because he is such a bully. I was surprised to hear Lucas say that Kevin had feelings like the rest of us. Lucas has a compassionate side. If I ever have a boyfriend, I would want him to be like Lucas!

Hailey slid the journal under her pillow and propped the pillow against the headboard so she could read *The Lion the Witch and the Wardrobe* by C. S. Lewis. Neko got up, stretched and rubbed his head against the book cover, looking for attention. Hailey scratched Neko behind the ears which started Neko purring like a small motor. After a few moments, Hailey stopped and Neko curled up next to Hailey's leg. Hailey was finishing the chapter with the talking animals when she fell asleep.

☼ ☼ ☼

"Wake up Hailey. We need to talk."

"What do you want Neko?"

"I found some big mice in the backyard. Do you want me to give them to your snake?"

"I don't have a snake!" said Hailey. "You know I hate snakes!"

Hailey looked around and saw she was in her backyard next to her pool. Neko was sitting on the patio table with a mouse in his mouth. The mouse was still wiggling, trying to free itself from the cat. Then Hailey saw a snake coiled up on the cement patio. She screamed for Lucas to help her, but no sound came out of her mouth.

"Hailey," said Lucas. "You look like you could use a little help."

Surprised to hear that familiar voice, Hailey turned around and saw Lucas standing there with a chameleon on his shoulder!

"Yes! Get rid of that snake!" pleaded Hailey.

Hailey quickly got behind Lucas so he was between her and the snake. Lucas had something in his hand, but she couldn't see what it was. Lucas raised his hand and pointed at the snake. A red beam of light came out of Lucas's finger like he was shooting the snake with a laser. The snake split into two snakes and they started slithering toward Lucas and Hailey. Lucas fired his laser finger again at the snakes and they split into four snakes. Each time they split, the snakes grew larger until they were as tall as Hailey and Lucas.

"Lucas, kill them!" cried Hailey. "You know how much I hate snakes!"

Hailey realized that the snakes were now yelling at them. It sounded like they were angry about something.

"Give it to us!" demanded the snakes. "We need to stay alive!"

Lucas and Hailey stepped backward in fear. Lucas seemed to be adjusting something in his hand. He then held up the palm of his hand as if to signal the snakes to stop.

"Stop!" commanded Lucas to the snakes.

To her surprise, Hailey saw the snakes actually stop—but only long enough to look at each other and laugh at Lucas. The four snakes turned their attention back to the Lucas and Hailey and continued move within striking distance. Standing behind Lucas, Hailey saw the chameleon on Lucas's shoulder stand on its hind legs and address the snakes.

"As one reptile to another, I suggest that you heed my master's warning and return to the hole from which you came."

"We just want to be friends with Hailey and Lucas. We need their power so we can stay alive. Please don't send us back into the dark," begged one of the snakes to Prescott.

"These snakes are not to be trusted," warned Prescott. "Lucas, send them back to their cave."

Immediately, a bright light radiated from Lucas's hand. The light grew brighter and brighter until the snakes disappeared in a puff of smoke.

"Thank you Lucas," said Hailey with a huge sigh of relief.

Then she looked at the chameleon on Lucas's shoulder and asked, "Are you the chameleon that Lucas found in his yard?"

"Yes, I am indeed. My name is Prescott and it is so nice to meet you Hailey." replied Prescott. "I heard that Lucas saved you from being run over by a big truck."

"How did you know?" asked Hailey. "That was supposed to be a secret."

"Heroic deeds like that are hard to be kept a secret," chimed in Neko. "Even I knew that—and I am just a cat."

Neko surprised Hailey when he hopped down from the patio table, ran to her and jumped up into her arms. Neko then looked at Prescott and said, "It is a great honor to meet the master chameleon. There has been chatter in the cat community that you had moved in with Lucas."

"Yes, Lucas is a fine young man," replied Prescott. "You must know that your keeper, Hailey, is an extraordinary young woman. Be watchful of her. She is destined to do wonderful things."

"I will," assured Neko.

Hailey was amazed with the conversation between these two animals and equally amazed that she could understand them.

"Lucas, what are you doing here?" asked Hailey.

"I came when you called me," said Lucas.

Hailey looked confused, "Did you bring Lucas here, Prescott?"

"No," replied Prescott, "he brought *me* here so you and I could talk."

"You want to talk to me? What do we need to talk about?"

"You need to help Lucas. He has some secrets and a lot of bad people want to harm him and take away his power," answered Prescott.

"What can I do?" asked Hailey.

"You need to be a friend and trust him. He has a good heart, but does not always think things through."

"Hey guys, I'm standing right here!" protested Lucas.

"Of course you are," said Prescott. "And that is where you need to stand. You need to stand for what is right."

"Hailey, can you keep a secret?" asked Prescott.

"Of course I can," replied Hailey. "I keep all my secrets locked in my vault."

Suddenly, they were back in Hailey's room as she pointed to a large floor-to-ceiling vault door in the wall of her room and said, "I am sure I can keep any secret Lucas has if it will protect him."

"Wonderful!" said Prescott. "There will be many secrets between you and Lucas. I am sure that you and he will make a good team and protect each other."

☼ ☼ ☼

As Prescott's voice trailed off, Hailey heard Neko meowing loudly and awoke to see him above her on the window sill again.

"That was a really strange dream, Neko," said Hailey. "It seemed so real though. You were in my dream and you were talking to me. Lucas was there and so was his chameleon. You and the chameleon were having quite a conversation. You talked as if you had a lot of respect and admiration for the chameleon. Is he really that special?"

Neko jumped down to the bed and pawed at the pile of stuffed animals. He pulled out a stuffed animal from the bottom of the pile that Hailey had forgotten. He picked up a stuffed chameleon and dropped it in Hailey's lap, and—as if to answer Hailey, said, "Meow!"

Hailey was astonished! She wondered if it was possible if Neko really could understand her.

"Did you really understand me, Neko?" asked Hailey expectantly.

"Meow."

TWELVE

Ranger, the Talking Dog

---

*We can learn to love unconditionally
from a dog. They look at our hearts.*

It didn't take long for the news to get around
school that Lucas had saved Hailey, and Miss
Harrison made a point of thanking him in class.
After school, Lucas stayed behind until all of the
others had left.

"Miss Harrison," said Lucas, "I was kind of
embarrassed today. I told Hailey that I didn't want
to make a big deal out of it."

"I'm sorry, Lucas, I had no idea."

"That's okay," said Lucas. "Can I talk with you
about something else?"

"What is it?" asked Miss Harrison.

"Kevin Cherno is sometimes a bully and he doesn't like me very much."

"Has he done anything to hurt you?" asked Miss Harrison.

"Well, he has splashed water on me and let the air out of my tires. I've seen him push Trevor and hide his backpack. He has also tripped Alex and some boys in another class. Somehow he does it to make it look like an accident. Miss Harrison, why does he do things like that?"

"That's a tough question to answer. There may be several reasons," said Miss Harrison thoughtfully. "Most often, bullies learn that kind of behavior at home either from parents or from an older brother or sister. Sometimes they learn to be a bully from their friends. The bully is often someone who feels powerless because of a family situation and finds ways to have power over others. A bully might feel he has no control over his life and he's desperate to be in control. Sometimes it's because they do not feel love from others, and maybe it's their way of getting attention. I know that Kevin's parents are divorced and he lives with his mother and older brother. We don't know all the reasons why someone is a bully, but it could be that they are angry about something or even afraid of something. It's usually connected to how a person feels about themselves."

Miss Harrison looked at Lucas and asked, "Are you afraid he might hurt you?"

"Oh no," said Lucas, "I used to be afraid of him, but not anymore. I'm sure he will not hurt me, but I'm concerned that someone else might get hurt."

Miss Harrison was quite surprised at Lucas's response. She had noticed a change in Lucas over the past few weeks. He seemed more confident and even a little more mature.

"Sometimes when a person is hurt, he wants to hurt back," said Miss Harrison. "A mature person will stop and try to figure out why that person is trying to hurt them. If you are concerned about helping Kevin, I would suggest that you find out what he likes or what he is good at and give him some honest complements. He might resist a little at first, but I'm sure he will appreciate your interest even if he doesn't show it."

To help Lucas feel more at ease, Miss Harrison said, "I'll watch the situation in class and on the school grounds to see if there is anything I need to do to help. And if necessary, I will send a note home to Kevin's mother." Lucas thanked Miss Harrison and headed home.

Prescott had told Lucas that over time, he would develop a connection to the Power Ring and would be able to use telekinetic power to turn the pointer to the desired power and squeeze the crystal with just his mind. This had become helpful when quick action was needed.

As Lucas was nearing his house, he saw a dog chasing a cat across the lawn toward the street. He also saw a car on a collision course with the cat and the dog. He thought quickly on how to stop the dog. He used the telekinetic power to turn the pointer to the Three Arrows and then with his mind, quickly slid a trash can at the curb in front of the dog, so he would either stop or run into it. The dog let out a loud yelp when he ran into the can, which saved him from running into the street and being hit by the car. The car swerved to miss the cat, so both the dog and cat were safe.

Lucas ran to the dog just as it was getting up. He kneeled down and let the dog smell the back of his hand and then began stroking the dog's head. The dog had a collar so maybe it would have a tag with the name and address of the owner. The dog looked familiar and the tag showed that the dog's name was Ranger.

"Oh, great!" said Lucas out loud, "I just saved Kevin Cherno's dog!"

Lucas quickly realized that this just might be the opportunity he needed to change Kevin's feelings toward him, so he headed home to talk with his mom. He held onto Ranger's collar and walked the one block to his house.

When Lucas got home, he told his mom that he stopped Kevin's dog from chasing a cat into the street and from getting run over by a car. He asked if he could take the dog to Kevin's house and explain how he found him.

His mom asked, "Isn't that the boy who's not nice to you?"

"I talked with Miss Harrison about Kevin, and she thinks that he might be a bully because he's angry at something or maybe someone in his family was a bully to him. If I take his dog home and explain how I found him, maybe he won't be mean to me anymore."

"Where does he live?" asked his mother.

"He lives in a house on the other side of the footpath bridge," replied Lucas.

"Okay, but be careful and come right home, we have to go to the store before your dad comes home from work." said his mom.

Lucas ran to get Prescott and the mesh pack and then untied Ranger from the garden hose. The hose was the only thing he could find to prevent Ranger from running in the street again.

As they walked toward Kevin's house, Lucas heard Prescott ask,

"Ranger, why are you limping?"

Lucas was surprised that Prescott was talking with Ranger, but even more surprised to hear the dog's response.

"I was chasing a cat and this big green thing moved right in my way. I smashed my nose and hurt my paw. Then this nice person took me to his house

and tied me up. It looks like we are going to my master's home now."

"Yes, we are going to your home," said Prescott. *"My keeper is a fine young man, and it is my duty to protect him. You should too."*

"I will protect him, too." said Ranger.

As Lucas walked up to the front porch, the door swung open and Kevin came out and angrily said, "What are you doing with my dog?"

Before Lucas could answer, Ranger ran to Kevin and jumped up on him and ran back to Lucas and jumped on him and licked his face and then back to Kevin. Ranger's tail was wagging wildly and that seemed to calm Kevin. Lucas explained that he stopped Ranger from chasing a cat into the street in front of a moving car. Lucas was careful to leave out the part about moving the trash can. Kevin had been ready to get angry at Lucas, but all he said was, "Oh. Okay. Thanks."

Lucas asked, "What kind of dog is Ranger?"

"Ranger is a Border Collie. I got him from my dad on my eighth birthday," replied Kevin.

"Does he do any tricks?" asked Lucas.

"Sure," said Kevin. "Watch this."

Kevin picked up a Frisbee on the porch and slapped it against his leg, calling to Ranger. Ranger lowered his head down with his rear up in the air and barked once, waiting for Kevin to toss it. He tossed the Frisbee slowly into the wind. Ranger ran after it, jumping about three feet into the air grabbing it with his teeth. Not only had Lucas secretly seen that before, he had even seen Ranger floating in mid air!

"That's so cool to see Ranger jumping and catching the Frisbee," said Lucas.

"*Lucas, would you please introduce me to Kevin?*" asked Prescott.

He wasn't sure why Prescott asked to be introduced, but Lucas had learned to trust him.

"Kevin, let me introduce you to a friend of mine," said Lucas as he sat on the lawn. He lifted Prescott out of the shoulder pack and held him in the palm of his hand.

"Kevin, this is my friend, Prescott. He's a veiled chameleon. Prescott, this is my friend Kevin," He surprised himself by calling Kevin his friend.

"Hello, Prescott. This is my dog, Ranger. He's a very smart Border Collie," said Kevin. "Ranger, say hello to Prescott."

Ranger stepped closer until his nose touched Prescott, then sat down and barked once.

"That's amazing!" exclaimed Kevin. "It's almost as if they could talk to each other."

Lucas had been thinking about his conversation with Miss Harrison, and since Kevin seemed to be calm, he decided to ask him a question.

"Kevin, sometimes you act like a bully and I was wondering if you know why?"

Kevin was surprised at the question and started to get angry, but then remembered that Lucas had gone out of his way to save Ranger. Kevin knew that Lucas was right. He was a bully.

"I don't know,' said Kevin shrugging his shoulders. "Since I moved here, I haven't really made any friends. Ranger is the only real friend I have. I don't know how to make friends and maybe I'm just trying to get some attention, to get noticed."

Lucas said, "I don't think that bothering or hurting someone is a good way to get attention."

"No, probably not," replied Kevin.

"If you want, we can start tossing a Frisbee during recess. Maybe we can work together on the book report assignment or something," said Lucas.

"I guess that would be okay," said Kevin, trying to hide the fact that he was secretly pleased. "Yes, I would like that."

Lucas put Prescott on the lawn and he and Kevin took turns tossing the Frisbee and having Ranger catch it in midair. After a few minutes, Lucas remembered that he had told his mom he would be right home.

"Kevin, I have to go home. I forgot my mom is waiting for me so we can go to the store."

"Okay. Hey! Thanks for bringing Ranger home and introducing me to Prescott."

As Lucas placed Prescott into the shoulder pack and turned to go, Prescott said, "*I do not think you will have any more trouble from Kevin.*"

THIRTEEN

Rescued From Fire

> *You will never know how strong you are*
> *until being strong is your only choice.*

Things had been a lot different over the next few weeks at school between Lucas and Kevin. Although they did not become close friends, there was a quiet truce between them. Kevin did not bother Lucas, and they even found they had a few things in common. They worked together and they each got an A on the book report assignment.

One evening, as Lucas turned out the light and climbed into bed, Prescott asked, *"Have you been listening to your heart?"*

"I think so," replied Lucas, "except for that time in the library when I was a bully to Kevin.

When I saved Hailey and Ranger a few weeks ago, I made some really quick decisions, but I think my heart helped me decide. What about the other symbols on the ring? When will you teach me about those?"

"All in good time, my eager young friend. You have been one of my brightest students, and you will accomplish great things in your life. But for now, be patient. There are a few more things you need to learn."

"What do I need to learn?" asked Lucas.

"You will know them when you learn them. Now go to sleep," replied Prescott.

☼ ☼ ☼

Lucas looked forward to the week at school when he was the classroom "Student of the Week." During that week, he had certain classroom privileges, as well as a Share Day. Lucas got to assist with the morning announcements over the PA system and was invited to eat lunch with his teacher. He was most excited about his Share Day. He wanted to bring Prescott to school, which he had arranged with Miss Harrison and Prescott for Thursday that week. Lucas brought Prescott to school and told his class how he found Prescott on the sidewalk in front of his house and about the kind woman who let Lucas keep the chameleon. He explained how chameleons eat and even brought some crickets to school to show the class. Several of the students wanted to hold Prescott and Lucas was considering it.

"*That is not a good idea, Lucas,*" cautioned Prescott. "*It is time to put me back in the cage.*"

Lucas decided to have some fun with the class and pretended to have a conversation with Prescott.

"What's that, Prescott? Did you say to put you back in the cage to eat some crickets?"

Lucas turned to the class and said, "As you can see, Prescott and I talk all the time. He just told me that he's hungry and wants to go back in the cage and get some crickets for lunch."

The class erupted into giggles. Lucas placed Prescott back into his cage and the entire class watched with anticipation as Prescott quickly snatched up the crickets with his long tongue. There was a lot of commotion from the children because they all wanted a close look at Prescott eating the crickets. After Prescott had grabbed the last cricket, Miss Harrison saw that it was time to head out to the garden.

Thursday was the day Miss Harrison's class worked in the school garden. Each class was responsible for a portion of the garden, and they all wanted their plants in the garden to do well. There were other schools in the area that had gardens, but Lucas's school had an award-winning-garden. Miss Harrison's class was responsible for the sunflowers and the carrots. Half of the class worked on weeding

around the carrots and the other half were working on the sunflowers.

They had planted the tall variety of sunflowers and Lucas's group was putting some bamboo stakes near each plant to support the heavy blossom.

That's when they heard the fire alarm. Miss Harrison had helped the class through several fire drills, which were usually announced beforehand. This might be the real thing! It had been a warm May and the dry desert winds were starting early. In Southern California, it is common to have wildfires in the hills, but to have one this early in the year was different. Lucas remembered his Uncle Brett telling the story of being on the ridge with the fire all around. As he thought about the fireman that died and his family, an overwhelming fear came over Lucas. He was thinking about his uncle when someone from the school office ran out to the garden.

"Miss Harrison! Miss Harrison! This is not a drill! You need to get all of the children to the far corner of the soccer field."

Lucas thought he could hear the sirens in the distance and he saw smoke coming from the cafeteria near his classroom. Some of the students were already coming out of the school buildings.

That's when he heard Prescott. *"Lucas, are you going to come get me? I am still in the classroom. Besides, there is someone else still in the building that you need to help!"*

Prescott had become Lucas's best friend in such a short time, and he wanted to go get him. But his fear of fire was so powerful that he just froze.

Then he heard Prescott's voice again. *"Lucas, I know that you have a fear of fire, but you need to trust me. You need to trust yourself."*

Every time he trusted Prescott, Lucas was able to accomplish what was needed. In spite of his fear, Lucas knew what he needed to do. Asking Miss Harrison if he could get Prescott wouldn't go well, so he went off by himself and ducked behind some bushes. He wasn't sure if he should try to stop time or be invisible. He chose to let the firemen do their job because he did not know how big of an area would be affected by stopping time. He turned the ring to the Double-S and squeezed the crystal imagining a curtain surrounding him and hiding him from everyone.

He was now invisible and started running back to the classroom as everyone else was walking away from the building. He actually had to run around the students so they wouldn't bump into him. Everyone else was walking away from the danger and Lucas was running right into it.

He got to his classroom and found the door had been locked. He ran around to the other side of the building where there were windows, hoping one would be open, but they were all locked as well. His eyes started to burn as the wind was blowing the smoke between the buildings and he started to cough. He had to get Prescott! He released the crystal, becoming visible again. He quickly turned the ring to the Three Arrows and focused on the window lock and willed it open.

He could hear Prescott in his head say, *"It's about time! I was getting just a little concerned that something might have happened to you. We need to hurry!"*

The window was hinged at the top and Lucas pulled it open with just enough room to climb up and squeeze through. He grabbed the shoulder pack from his desk as he ran to the counter at the back of the room. He pulled Prescott from the cage and slid him into his shoulder pack. As he ran for the door, he heard a voice in his head—but it wasn't Prescott's voice this time. It was his Uncle Brett. He remembered him saying, "If the door is hot, don't open it." As he neared the door he could feel some heat and wondered how the fire had gotten there so quickly.

He turned around to head for the windows and saw that the bushes between the buildings had also caught fire. Just then the fire sprinklers came on and Lucas was soaked within a few seconds. Again he heard Uncle Brett's voice telling him, "In a fire, you look for all possible escape routes." Lucas remembered there were connecting doors between the classrooms and ran toward the First and Second Grade doors. Once he was through one room, he ran toward the next door away from the direction of the fire. When he got to the last room, the fire alarm was directly above him.

The noise was so loud he put his hands up to cover his ears. As he did, he tilted his head

toward the ground where he was surprised to see a little girl sitting on the floor crying. Then he remembered Prescott saying there was someone else who needed help.

Lucas rushed over to her, and in a loud voice, asked, "What are you still doing here?"

"I went to the bathroom, and when I came out everyone was gone. I didn't know what to do or where to go. I'm scared!"

"What's your name?"

"Anna," she replied.

"Well, Anna, my name is Lucas, and you're going to be safe." Lucas wasn't sure of that himself, but he needed to be strong for little Anna.

Lucas took her by the hand and said, "We have to get out of here!"

They ran for the door, and Lucas felt for any heat. There was none, so he opened it slowly. He had gone far enough away from the fire and saw a large stream of water coming over the top of the building that was directed at the flames. Lucas knew that the firemen had arrived and they were doing what they were trained to do.

Lucas opened the door all the way and turned to run away from the fire, but he had forgotten that there was an eight-foot chain link fence. It was meant to keep vandals out, but now it was trapping them in! He thought about putting Anna on his back and climbing, since she was too little to climb by herself.

"Prescott, can you help us?"

"Who is Prescott," asked Anna.

Lucas didn't answer.

Lucas heard Prescott in his head say, *"You have all the power you need in the ring. Just trust yourself."*

Lucas thought to himself that being invisible wouldn't get them over the fence. Even if I stopped time, he thought, we still have to climb. Can I use telekinesis to get us over?

With smoke swirling around his head, Lucas could feel the heat from the fire. He could feel his own fear rising, causing his muscles to lock and his mind to go blank. He was frozen in fear and stood motionless as he stared at the fence—until he heard Anna's voice.

"Are we going to die?" That brought Lucas out of his trance. He shook his head hard to break himself out of the feeling of being powerless.

"No! We are not going to die!" exclaimed Lucas firmly. "We are going to get out of here!"

Lucas knew that the firemen might be coming around the building soon. He did not want to hang around to see them or be seen by anyone else. Lucas had been able to move objects but could he move himself and Anna? Lucas decided to follow Prescott's advice and trust himself. He had to try something new.

An idea started to take shape in his mind. He turned the ring to the Three Arrows. Lucas was about a foot taller than Anna and as he looked down at her he said, "I am going to get us out of here Anna, but you have to trust me and do exactly what I tell you."

"All right, Lucas," replied Anna.

Lucas could see the fear in her eyes that were still wet with tears. Her clothes and hair were soaked with water from the fire sprinklers.

"Anna, I want you to wrap your arms around me very tight like this," said Lucas as he pulled her arms around to his back. "Put your face against my shirt, stand on my feet, and close your eyes as tight as you can."

She followed his instructions and, after making sure his shoulder pack with Prescott was securely on his shoulder, Lucas wrapped his arms around Anna. Then, using the power of telekinesis, Lucas imagined them all rising in the air and floating over the fence.

At first, Lucas felt a little unstable and off balanced. He pushed the fear of fire out of his mind and imagined the fear flying into the flames behind him. The faith that Lucas had that he could do this was rewarded. If anyone had been watching, they would have seen something amazing! Lucas, Anna and Prescott rose slowly to the height of the building, floated about fifteen feet past the fence and then descended slowly to the ground with a smooth landing. Lucas looked around quickly to make sure no one saw them.

Once they were on the ground, Lucas released his grip on Anna and said, "You can open your eyes now. We need to hurry and run to the soccer field."

Anna's teacher was frantic when she discovered that one of her students was missing. Two firefighters got the assignment to search for Anna. They were coming toward the school when they saw Lucas and Anna come running around the corner of the building toward them. One of the firemen scooped Anna up in his arms and carried her over to her teacher. Lucas walked along beside him and then turned to join his class.

Miss Harrison came up and put her arm around his shoulder and walked him a short distance from the class. She noticed the shoulder pack he was now wearing and knew that Lucas had gone back to the classroom to rescue Prescott.

"Lucas, you were supposed to stay with the class," said Miss Harrison sternly. "Do you realize how dangerous it was to go back for your chameleon?"

"Miss Harrison, I am sorry, but I *had* to save Prescott. He is very special to me and I needed to go back to get him.

"When I was leaving the building I heard someone crying and found Anna in her classroom. I knew I couldn't wait for the firemen and I had to get her to safety as quickly as possible."

Miss Harrison was glad that Anna and Lucas were safe. She had taught a lot of children, but never anyone like Lucas and decided that there must be something very extraordinary about Lucas and his chameleon. Her heart softened, and she thanked Lucas for saving Anna.

"Please stay with your class now, Lucas, until your mother comes and you are released to go home."

Lucas stepped a few feet away from the others so he could be alone with Prescott. He found a branch on a bush and pulled Prescott out of the shoulder pack, so the chameleon could climb onto a branch.

Lucas looked at Prescott and said, "Your collar has the same symbols that are on the Power Ring. Do you have the same power on your collar that is on the ring?"

"I do indeed."

"Then could you have saved yourself?" asked Lucas.

"Yes, I could have saved myself, and I could have saved little Anna. But you needed to find out for yourself what you were capable of doing, Lucas. You will never know how strong you are until being strong is the only choice you have."

"So this was a test." said Lucas.

"Yes, Lucas, it was. You needed to learn for yourself just how strong you are. Do you remember asking what you needed to learn before I teach you more about the Power Ring? This was one of those lessons. You have proven to me and to yourself how you will use the unique powers you have been given. You also showed your true character by what you were willing to do. I am very pleased with your actions today," said Prescott.

"Thank you," replied Lucas with a sigh. He was glad it was over.

Lucas put Prescott back into the shoulder pack and looked over in the parking lot for his mother where the parents were arriving to pick up their children. Lucas finally spotted his mom there, holding Gavin's hand. Lucas pointed them out to Miss Harrison who released Lucas to be with his family, and he quickly walked toward them. In the crowd, standing behind his mom, Lucas thought he saw a woman who looked like Katrina. When he got closer, the woman smiled directly at Lucas, and he was sure. The same glow he saw when he stood on her porch seemed even brighter.

Lucas's mom, Hannah, reached out and drew Lucas into a tight hug, checking to make sure he was not hurt. But before she could ask Lucas about the fire, and why he was so wet, Hannah was distracted by Gavin and turned to see what he wanted.

Lucas looked behind his mom and saw Katrina smiling at him. It was then that he noticed that noise level was dropping. Suddenly, the world around Lucas became frozen in time. Only he, Prescott and Katrina were moving.

"Hello Lucas," said Katrina. "I see you have learned well from Prescott."

"Hey, did you just stop time?" asked Lucas.

"No, that was Prescott," said Katrina. "That was a very brave thing you did by going back inside the school building to save Prescott and Anna."

"I needed to save my friend. Prescott has helped me see that I can do a lot more than I thought I could," said Lucas.

"Today you saved Prescott and Anna, but there was someone else that you saved as well," said Katrina.

"I did? Who was that?"

"You saved yourself."

"Oh. I guess so! I did save myself from the fire."

"Yes, you saved yourself from the fire," said Katrina, "but you also saved yourself from your fear.

Your fear of fire has held you captive and today you have freed yourself from being its prisoner."

"Wow! I never thought of it that way," said Lucas. "Thanks to you, Prescott is the best friend I've ever had!"

"You are so welcome. You two make a good team," said Katrina.

"When you gave Prescott to me, you knew he was a magical chameleon and you knew about the Power Ring, didn't you?"

"Yes I did," replied Katrina. "I knew that Prescott had chosen you because he believed in you and your ability to learn to use the Power Ring. Lucas, I need to go now, and you need to be with your family."

"Will I see you again?" asked Lucas.

"I'm sure we will meet again. Goodbye for now—and keep listening to Prescott," added Katrina.

Lucas could hear the sounds around him start to increase. As he watched Katrina turn and walk away, he was grabbed from behind by his mother and brother and given another big hug.

As she made her way through the crowds, Katrina had a private conversation with Prescott.

"*Does Lucas know yet? Does he know what he is?*" asked Katrina.

"*No, he does not know.*"

"*When will he be told?*" asked Katrina.

"We will tell him in the coming weeks," replied Prescott.

"He is still very young. Will he be ready?"

"He is a fast learner, and he is willing to listen to those who have fought this battle before. Never before has there been one with the birthright— until Lucas."

"I know," said Katrina. *"That is why I am so hopeful. But the enemy will know soon as well."*

"Then we must all stand beside Lucas and protect him until he has the power to fulfill his destiny."

FOURTEEN

The Promise

Everyone deserves someone who
makes them look forward to tomorrow.

Hailey Sinclair lived right behind the school, so her mother was one of the first parents to take her child home. Hailey and her mother were standing on patio chairs watching the fire over the fence from their backyard when the phone rang. Hailey's mom went into the house to answer it and Hailey continued to watch the fire and all of the commotion at the school. That's when she saw Lucas. He had his arms wrapped around a little girl and they floated through the air over the chain link fence.

Hailey thought back to the day Lucas saved her from being run over by the trash truck. He had told

124

her he had stopped time. She thought he was just being silly, but what she saw today was something that was just as impossible. Right then, she was determined to find out what was going on with Lucas and what secrets he might be hiding.

Because of the fire, and the fact that there was only one week of school left, the school district ended the school year and officially sent the kids home for the summer. The next day, Hailey asked if she could go to Lucas's house to talk about the fire. Her mom agreed, and Hailey called Lucas to see if she could come over.

Lucas and Hailey were in his backyard that afternoon, hanging out on the tire swing, talking about the school fire, getting out of school early, and what they both had planned for the summer.

Then, the conversation slowed, and they were quiet for awhile.

Hailey said abruptly, "I saw you yesterday during the fire. I saw you help the little girl."

"Well I just did what anyone would do," replied Lucas.

"No. I mean I saw you holding the little girl with your arms wrapped her! I saw the two of you floating over the fence!"

"I don't know what you are talking about!" protested Lucas.

"Lucas, when you saved me from the trash truck, you said that you just stopped time and I thought you were joking. But I saw you and the little girl lift off of the ground and float over the fence. Then, after you came down, you ran around the building to the field. I was not *in* the soccer field. I was at home looking over my fence and I saw you. So just tell me, how did you do that?"

"I guess some invisible angels picked us up and carried us over."

"Lucas Lightfoot," exclaimed Hailey. "I'm serious! Tell me how you did that!"

Then with a smirk, Hailey teased, "I may just have to tell everyone your secret and say I saw you float over the fence with that little girl."

"And who is going to believe you? I'll just say that I carried Anna on my back and I climbed over the fence," said Lucas with a grin.

Hailey groaned with frustration. "Why won't you tell me?"

Lucas thought for a moment and listened to his heart. He then heard Prescott in his head.

"Lucas, you trusted yourself yesterday and what you did was very heroic. Tell Hailey that you have been granted some special powers because of your honest heart. Tell her that you will tell her the secret IF she will promise that she will keep the secret between just the two of you."

"Well?" said Hailey. "Are you going to tell me?"

"Hailey," began Lucas, "I suppose because of my honest heart, I have been granted a gift of special powers that are unlike anything I could have ever imagined. I can tell you about them only if you promise to keep everything I tell you a secret between us."

"I can keep a secret," said Hailey.

"I thought that the garbage truck incident was going to be our secret."

"I promise, I did not say a word," pleaded Hailey. "Emily Parker overheard our conversation after you saved me and she told Miss Harrison. Miss Harrison called and talked to my mom and it grew from there."

With a solemn tone, Lucas said, "The secret I have can only be used for good to help others. You have to understand that if the wrong people find out, I may lose my ability or it can be taken away. Or worse yet, the gift might be stolen from me."

Hailey could see the intense worry on his face, and she could hear the seriousness in his voice when Lucas said he was afraid of losing what he called "the gift."

"I know," said Hailey. "I believe you."

"How do you know?" questioned Lucas.

"I had a dream. You, Prescott and my cat Neko were in my dream. I was being attacked by snakes and you killed them with some sort of bright light. In my dream, Prescott told me that I need to keep your secret and not tell anyone. He said that there are some bad people who want to hurt you."

"Did Prescott say who they were?"

"No."

"Did Prescott say anything else in your dream?" asked Lucas.

"He said that I was to be a friend and to trust you," said Hailey. "He also said that we make a good team. Lucas, I make you a solemn promise that I can be trusted to keep your secret."

"Pinky swear?"

"Pinky swear!" declared Hailey, as they hooked little fingers together.

"All right, I will tell you, but not here and not now. It's a long story. We are leaving soon to visit my grandpa this weekend for his birthday. When I get back, we can get together and I will tell you the entire story."

About the Authors

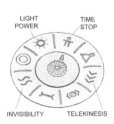

LIGHT POWER   TIME STOP

INVISIBILITY   TELEKINESIS

Hugo Haselhuhn lives in San Luis Obispo County and has a passion to create a positive influence for good in the lives of others. Hugo has incorporated lessons into this story that can help children with their emotional growth and relationships as the readers learn through the eyes and experiences of the characters.

This book began as a request from his co-author and grandson, Luke Cowdell, who wanted help in writing a "chapter book". Luke was seven years-old

at the time he asked Grandpa for help. Luke is an avid reader with an active imagination. He is also a deep thinker and asks questions seemingly beyond his years.

NOW AVAILABLE...

Lucas and Hailey continue the adventure with new powers, new challenges, new friends and a new adversary in the second book in the series, *Lucas Lightfoot and the Water Tomb*. The book is available at www.lucaslightfoot.com.

From Lucas Lightfoot and the Water Tomb

Not Alone Any More

A friend is someone who understands
your past, believes in your future, and
accepts you just the way you are.

The sky was very blue that day in late May and the white clouds reminded Lucas of popcorn. It was sunny—that is, until a menacing shadow, moving incredibly fast, slithered across the sky and covered the backyard at the home of Lucas's grandfather. Thinking the sudden shadow was from one of the clouds, Lucas looked up to see a dark shape covering the sun.

It wasn't a cloud at all but a dark form that quickly came down on top of Lucas and enclosed him in a dark mist. Lucas started shivering as he was surrounded by the shape. His nose was attacked by the smell of rotten eggs, and he found it very difficult to breathe.

He yelled to his grandfather, but no sound came out of his mouth. Each breath caused his nose and throat to hurt like the stings of a thousand bees. Lucas felt as if he were bound by an invisible rope. He couldn't move his arms to fight off his attacker or move his feet to run. He felt himself being lifted off the ground and pulled away.

His grandfather turned around and reached out for Lucas, but it was too late. Lucas saw his grandfather and the backyard getting smaller as he felt himself being pulled up and away very fast. The last thing Lucas remembered was seeing Prescott on his grandfather's shoulder, and there was a bright

glow coming from Prescott's collar. After that, everything went dark.

To discover what happens to Lucas and who, or *what*, took him, download the entire first chapter from Lucas Lightfoot and the Water Tomb, by going to: www.lucaslightfoot.com/LLWT/chapterone

CPSIA information can be obtained
at www.ICGtesting.com
Printed in the USA
BVHW04s0849250518
517346BV00001B/2/P